THE BOATWRIGHT

AND THE FISHERMEN

Gene R. Stark

New Harbor Press
Rapid City, SD

New Harbor Press
1601 Mt Rushmore Rd, Ste 3288
Rapid City, SD 57701
www.newharborpress.com

Ordering Information:
Quantity sales. Special discounts are available on quantity purchases by corporations, associations, and others. For details, contact the "Special Sales Department" at the address above.

The Boatwright and the Fishermen/Stark —1st ed.

ISBN 978-1-63357-425-0

First edition: 10 9 8 7 6 5 4 3 2 1

Contents

Prologue-1986, the Northwest shore of the Sea of Galilee

Fishermen Brothers

I wasn't sure I could take another step as the mud sucked at my boots. The unusual heat and humidity drained my efforts, yet the thought of finding anything exposed by the extended drought pushed me onward.

"Yuval," I shouted at my brother and pointed ahead, "there are several objects sticking out of the mud!"

In the distance, the Sea of Galilee glimmered in the sun as we trekked the mud flats on the edge of the great sea. The mud flats were created by the long dry spell and were a ripe hunting ground for ancient artifacts.

We slogged toward the objects now appearing almost as the ribs of a giant beast.

"It has the shape of an old boat that sank here long ago." Yuval, like myself had grown up fishing on the Sea of Galilee and recognized the form of a craft. We then knew it to be the remains of a boat, described as the type used by fishermen of the sea during the first century. Even now, after many centuries laying buried in the mud, it was evident that the boatwright who built it with only hand tools and much labor was a very skilled craftsman.

A presence of importance quickly enveloped us as we began to envision the boat from the remains in front of us.

"We must contact an archaeologist. This is the type of boat Jesus traveled in on Galilee," I pointed toward our Kibbutz Ginosar where we lived and followed the fishing traditions of generations of our family.

As we reached the dry shoreland the seabirds swirled and dived around us. We stopped to look back and Yuval looked at me, "Moshe, this is indeed a very important discovery."

The Boatwright and the Fishermen

Seabirds rise and dive
Twist and swirl in smoke-like flight,
By the diamonds in the morning light.
Constant rhythm of mallet-beats,
Punctuate the breeze and stones.
Holy boats and sacred fish,
Solemn men with sun burnt tones,
Constant rhythm of mallet-beats
Punctuate the breeze and sands
The boatwright meets the sea's demands.

CHAPTER 1

By the Sea (circa 30 A.D.)

I never imagined on the day I first saw him, that my boats would transport the Son of God. My little workplace clung to the gentle shore of Lake Galilee near the village called Magdala of the Fishers. I sat under my humble shelter as the gentle waves caressed the timeless fire-stones placed on the shore by the Creator thousands of years ago. The breakwater stopped any serious disruption as the fishermen mended their nets and cleaned the baskets that held the morning catch. The lake sparkled silvery-blue as a friendly zephyr caressed the clear waters. The smell of fish and freshwater vegetation were my constant companions, an odor that gave strange comfort to one who had grown up on these shores.

Although the sea has always been my solace, we lived in a time of turbulence. The Roman world ruled us and touched everything in our lives. Our existence seemed quiet, almost pristine, nestled by the blue waters of Galilee, yet our faith and the essence of Israel were touched by political undercurrents that pulsed through our minds and our very souls each day.

I knew them all, the folks who rose in the dark of the morning to set out and trust their fortunes to the fickle waters of the great lake. Rough, callused hands worked the sails and oars, cleaned and mended the nets, and sorted the catch. Dark, sinewy backs bent and stretched with the daily physical labor. Ohers who I knew were also of the commonest sort: sowing crops, harvesting grain, and trusting the land and climate to carry them through each season. Yet these common folks all came to see the hand of God more clearly than the learned scholars. I came to realize the power of the common, and the insurmountable strength of the people of the water and the soil of our holy land.

On that day in my memory the clear and fertile plain along the opposite shore stared green and lush with crop. Small fish broke the surface, chased by predators of the great inland sea. As I rested in the midday heat, my project stared out into its future life. My next boat to be launched soon upon the fertile waters would float sailors and fisherman to the farthest reaches of the lake. My occupation as a boat-builder was indeed satisfying as I saw the fruits of my workmanship carry fishermen to their daily pursuits. In fact, my demand had increased to the point that I needed additional help to meet my contracts.

As though they were white swirls of mist, I saw the seabirds dive and ascend; waves of white about a figure walking along the shore. The birds fluttered and dived as an almost holy veil of protection as the solitary man mapped his meticulous route along the great sea. Slowly he picked his way among the stones and shells, stopping often to gaze upon the blue water as the seabirds seemed to pave his way along the shore. Tunic and hair rippled in the breeze as he turned often to the hills behind as if drawn to the highlands, yet always brought back and caressed by the rippled water.

The path above the lake shore would have been much easier to travel, yet he chose the rocky lakeside shore. Perhaps the serenity of the lake or the need for serenity drew him. Maybe he had time to contemplate his next moves or maybe he knew his future and chose to take this day slowly, let its gentle hand calm his demeanor. Perhaps it was just his way, chosing to travel the difficult path. He approached my little occupation as if he had come to it often. He stopped on the shore, surveyed my latest project, turned to the fishermen who toiled, smiled with knowing countenance, and approached my shelter,

Although I had never met him, I recognized him as a seasoned woodworker as he caressed my woodworking tools with hardened and calloused hands and surveyed the framework of the boat I was building. He was in his twenties and his name had come to my attention as I inquired among other artisans of possible workers in my little trade. He was called Jesus and came from Nazareth. Having grown up in the woodworking trade, he seemed a possible prospect to help me expand my business.

The export of fish from our Lake Galilee had become a bustling business and it especially impacted our little town. Here the catch of many fishermen was dried, salted, and readied for export to various places in the Roman world. My little business was built upon the fishing industry. I built the boats used by the fishermen upon this inland sea. "Moshe's Boat Works" had risen to good standing and excellent reputation among the watermen who sailed my boats. My boats were especially designed for the fickle waters of Lake Galilee.

"Are you Moshe?" He asked straightforward in an almost knowing manner. His gaze encompassed me, looked into my inner thoughts and his eyes embodied a complete sincerity.

"I am he."

"Word has traveled to me that you seek someone who can work in wood. I am Jesus from Nazareth. I grew up in the carpentry business."

"Can you work in the precise measurements required to build a sound and reliable boat?"

"I can," and his eyes turned to the framework of a boat that I was constructing, "I have seen your boats on the lake; they are fine craft."

"I have contracts for several boats. I can pay you for your labor as they are completed and paid for."

"You are an honest man, I don't worry about the money."

So, it began as he entered my world by the sea, and drew me inextricably into His world.

I built boats with the greatest of care. Thirty-six spans long and ten spans wide. They were built to allow the fishermen to work in the shallows, but also navigate and withstand the treacherous wind storms that frequently blew across Galilee. They could be easily rowed and handled by a crew of four and were easily sailed in proper wind. Simple, yet strong and built for utility. Cedar was my preferred wood, with each board mortised and pegged. I preferred to use all wooden pegs to assure no leaks. Once my boats soaked in the fresh water of Galilee, they remained dry and trouble-free. My customers were men who knew the lake and knew how to make a profit from its abundant waters. They also knew good craftsmanship. Although my stature was small and I might not hold up to the hot sun and long days on a boat, my hands were cut and roughened from the constant work with wood-working tools and my fingers strong as the wooden pegs that held my boats together. I knew the work of fishermen and they respected my knowledge of boat construction.

We worked together, Jesus and I. His hands were strong, calloused in the places where the tools of the trade were held. I watched his steadiness as he held the ribs and cross-members in place as I carefully drilled and pegged them into permanence. We worked steadily in the cool of the early morning, completing the framework.

"This is good work, it is the toil I have come to know. I also know the men who sweat in the fishing boats to bring in a catch and I watch the farmers and shepherds who work the land to make a living." Jesus stopped for a moment to wipe the sweat from his face.

"We are the ones who make Israel strong and prosperous and of course we support the Roman Empire."

"Moshe, tell me of your family," his genuine and quiet demeanor drew my deepest thought.

"My family grew up by the Sea of Galilee. My father and brothers fish the waters."

"What brought you to the boat-building trade?"

"A neighbor took me to the highlands to the north and there I saw the cedar trees. In each one, I could see a boat. My neighbor was a carpenter and he envisioned a trade. I learned of boats from my father and brother. The skills I learned from my neighbor seemed to transfer to seafaring craft. I learned the design and knew from my growing up what fishermen need and want in a craft."

"You have perfected a plan for your boats."

"There is no perfection. Just as the priests sacrifice to God and yet we remain a sinful and oppressed people."

"The prophets point to a Messiah," he countered.

"Some say the Messiah has come. I have gone to listen to the Rebel; he proclaims that he will break free from the Roman oppression."

"Moshe, what is the meaning of the Prophets?"

"We will be delivered."

"In the meantime, you will build your boats and profit from the fishing trade?"

"I will make a living but the Roman taxes on our work oppress us all. Even to be allowed to build and sell my boats, I must buy a license. It will take a Messiah to free us from the Romans."

"The Messiah will deliver us in ways many do not yet understand."

I remember the conversation and it brings to mind the feeling I had for Levi, the tax collector. He extorted forty percent of my sale price on each boat. That was after he charged me for the license to build boats. Levi and his crew of thugs made it very clear to all businessmen and fishermen on the lake that either you comply with the tax or you might be subject to very unpleasant consequences. The outwardly mild-mannered Levi controlled a band of enforcers who made certain not a single fish was sold without proper taxation. My boats were carefully scrutinized as I sold them. Of course, I added to the price to make up some of the exorbitant rate.

"But you make a profit, don't you?" Jesus met my eyes with knowing compassion.

"As I said, I make a living," I replied.

"I will make it a point to visit Capernaum and observe the work of these agents of Herod," Jesus portrayed a genuine interest in knowing everyone.

Jesus stayed by the sea, camping out by the clear, blue waters. Often, he would sit for hours, seemingly entranced by the quiet waves. Eventually the rainy season set in and Jesus found a house in Capernaum.

Silver tribute rings upon the table,
Open-air collection
As heavy-handed thugs enable
Enforcement of the Empire rules.
Silver tribute rings upon the table,
They pay as they are able.
Messiah eyes forgive,
Let live
As silver tribute rings upon the table.

CHAPTER 2

Levi

From my youngest days, I was brought up to hate the tax collector. All I needed to know as a youth was that he stole our income. Hate is an easy thing until you get to know someone. Now I knew the man and his name was Levi. How could I not know him? I dealt with him on an almost daily basis. It is true that Levi took our money just like all the tax representatives. Levi represented the hated Romans. He collected our taxes. He did his job yet he searched for better things, and I found I could not hate Levi. To be certain Levi was a tough man and some of his associates are truly rough characters. It is a mean and hated business. Yet Levi was a meticulous keeper of records and had a keen connection to the people around him.

The tax was due on my next boat. Jesus and I had toiled long and hard to get it completed. Simon and Andrew were anxious to add a boat to their fishing business. They had grown up fishing on Galilee with their father and his hired help. Simon especially pushed hard for completion of the boat we were working on.

Jesus commented after one of Simon's visits to check on our progress, "Simon is surely a steady and driven person; he seems to push hard to get things done."

"I have known Simon since my youth. He gets more determined as he ages. Things can never get done fast enough to suit him."

I went to pay my tax upon completion of another boat.

"May I follow along?" Jesus asked as I left to go visit Levi.

"Come along and see how those who do the Romans' bidding operate."

I introduced Jesus to Levi. The tax collector commented in his causal, witty manner, "So you bring your workers to see the evils of my occupation?"

"There is no evil that cannot be forgiven and changed for the better," Jesus looked into Levi's eyes with stern compassion. At those words Levi remained silent, looking puzzled by Jesus' words.

"I need to see a bill of sale on your last boat," he said as he looked through me with sharp, dark eyes.

"You know by now what they sell for," I had learned to toy with him.

"The bill, Moshe," a hidden smile at my insolence.

It was my business, and of course I had to pass the cost of taxes onto my buyers. Levi knew that I knew how to make a profit.

"Don't you get tired of wrangling your fellow countrymen?" I prodded him.

"It's a living, Moshe."

"Have you heard the Rebel?" I changed the subject.

At my question, Levi's eyes darted about, to be sure none of his fellow tax collectors were within hearing.

"I have heard his message," the low, restrained response, met only my ears.

"Have you heard the Baptist?" I continued to harass him with dangerous questions.

"His message would condemn a sinner like me."

"As he says, 'Repent.' You could quit this sad business."

Only a sigh from Levi as he counted my coins and looked out to the glistening lake, where all our incomes originated. He turned from me to complete his meticulous recording of the day's transactions. His gift of language and passion for detail never ceased to amaze me.

"Levi, you could learn the boat-building trade, with your attention to detail."

"Perhaps it is an occupation that might one day save my soul, but I doubt my hands or back could endure the work."

"Listen to the prophet, he speaks of the Messiah."

"Perhaps he will deliver us all, but only the power of the true Messiah would turn my heart," Levi's glance to the sea seemed to rest his tense demeanor for a brief moment. My visits to Levi always left him looking to the sea.

Jesus and I headed back to the sea-side. Always looking ahead, especially as regarded my business, I thought about my need for help. I was now getting caught up on orders for boats, my need for extra help decreased.

"Your work has been excellent and a great help to me, but I am getting caught up on my projects," I commented in the late afternoon.

"Do not worry for me. I have work ahead of me that will soon occupy all of my time."

"Big building project in Nazareth?"

"Much of my work will actually be near Galilee."

"Then we will see each other often?" I thought I'd see more of his workmanship. Little did I realize the nature of his future occupation.

The next day Simon and Andrew came to take their new boat on its maiden voyage.

"So, you are ready to take possession of our boat?" I welcomed the brothers.

Simon, with his usual exuberance ran up and clasped my hand and embraced me, "Moshe, you have built us a beautiful boat. We will bring in many baskets of fish in this craft."

Andrew, tall, muscular, and dark from the sun, strode past to the boat, "It is a beautiful work of art."

"It is a fine and durable craft. Now we will join forces with the sons of Zebedee and together we will dominate these waters," Peter laid out the plan of the company.

"We often fish near John and James. When they locate large schools we too prosper as we fish alongside of them. Now we can search the waters more efficiently and we will all prosper." Andrew, the quieter of the brothers, yet the more practical, explained.

"You are a mighty fishing family," I agreed.

Peter then inquired, "Who is this Jesus of Nazareth who has helped you build this craft?"

"A carpenter from Nazareth, well-schooled in the trade. He is also one who looks to the coming of a Messiah. He, like you, has heard of John the Baptist."

"I am a follower of the Baptist. I have been cleansed in the River Jordan where he preaches," Andrew proclaimed.

"Andrew wants me to accompany him to see and hear the Baptist," Simon added, "and perhaps I too will follow John the Baptist."

"He speaks of the one to follow him. He prepares the way for the Messiah," Andrew grew excited.

My skepticism showed, "There have been many prophets and others who claimed to be the Messiah."

"Andrew says John preaches with a special authority. He proclaims that he is only paving the way for one much greater. We will find out soon as we leave our beloved Sea of Galilee to visit the desert and hear the Baptist."

"Keep me informed; surely we need a Messiah to rid us of the Roman scourge," I added.

"And the Roman taxes," Simon added. "In fact we need to pay Levi a visit to pay taxes on our last catch."

"Levi, a good man in his heart, but corrupted by the greed for Roman money," I added as we moved the new boat on rollers toward the water's edge.

The boat scraped on the gravel as we pushed it lightly onto the shimmering, clear water. The craft now floated lightly and perfectly level in the shallows. Its flat bottom and short draft allowed it to be navigated close to shore with little effort.

"Yuval," Simon shouted to one of his helpers, "come and handle an oar in our new craft."

The four of us took the boat out and rowed it easily along the shore, maneuvering it effortlessly in whatever patterns we wished.

"With a crew of just four, we can take this vessel anywhere on the lake with oars or sail. Moshe, you are a master of your craft."

"And now Simon, you will be the master of this craft," I replied as the small fish, the sardines of the common folks surfaced in abundance near the side of the boat.

These fishermen had invested their lives into their trade. I felt that nothing could separate men like Simon and Andrew from the water and fishing. I would learn that faith and passion trumped all else.

Steel upon steel rattles in the dark,
Murmurs by the flashing fires,
The Rebel prattles to his troops,
Taunting timid mercenary hires.
"Barabbas, Barabbas,"
Hungry, mutinous voices bark
As steel upon steel rattles in the dark;
Roman soldiers make their mark.

The Rebel

Perhaps I just needed a break from the waterfront on Galilee, or maybe my curiosity had finally pushed me to journey to Jerusalem, but I left my boat building for a pilgrimage to the south.

I have no great love for the busy city of Jerusalem but I had set my sights on Mt. Olivet on the outskirts of the city. The Mt. of Olives is a gathering place where ideas are exchanged and people express their hopes, dreams, and beliefs. I camped among the Olive trees at Gethsemane, shared fires with prophets and rebels, all who aspired to changing the world.

My curiosity led me to hear the Rebel. He spoke at a well-attended rally on The Mount. Barabbas was his name, his message was of insurrection, beating back the Romans by force. His cause was very belligerent and those who opposed him faced violence. I followed his message. It was a message I wanted to hear and many were excited by a person who would stand up against our oppressors. Yet I could not see this person as a Messiah. Isaiah spoke of the promised Messiah as one who "like a lamb is led to slaughter, and like a sheep that before its shearers is silent, so he opened not his mouth. He had done no violence and there was no deceit in his mouth." Isaiah 53:7, 9.

The Messiah was described in a much different way, his actions much different from those of Barabbas. Barabbas attracted large crowds and whipped them into a frenzy. Violence was sure to erupt as those crowds came into contact with Roman suppression.

Roman soldiers laughed at the political notions of Barabbas and his Zealot notions of overthrowing the occupying forces.

"Let him rattle on for a while; he will soon be imprisoned and probably crucified," one Roman captain told a group who had come to hear Barabbas. "You will see the foolishness of his intent." I stayed back from the boisterous group who surrounded Barabbas closely.

"We must take up arms and drive the occupiers from our holy land!" he spoke with fire and anger. Yet I could not see him as a Messiah. Isaiah spoke of a lamb, not a lion.

I went to a small fire in the garden where I camped and there I met Simon, one of the Zealot followers of Barabbas and his group.

"We must drive the Romans from our land and our holy city. God has ordained this land to belong to the Jews," Simon the Zealot spoke with passion.

"One of my fisherman friends on the Sea of Galilee follows John who preaches in the desert. Have you heard the message of John? He preaches repentance and forgiveness. He baptizes and tells us we must change our hearts. He says this is the only way we will once again possess the Kingdom of God." I countered.

"How does this free us from the Romans who suck the life-blood from our land?"

As we spoke, there arose a great uproar near the entrance of the garden. We heard the clash of steel and voices yelling in anger. There were screams and the shouting of orders by Roman soldiers. A figure rushed past our fire, carrying an unsheathed sword glistening with blood. Soldiers ran over our fire, pushing us both to the ground as they lumbered past us in heavy armor. Behind them there were torches and angry groups of people.

"It begins," Simon looked at me intently.

"But where will it end? There must be more than the endless fighting and rebellion. I have a desire to hear for myself what John preaches." I now felt the need for another foray from my peaceful seaside business.

"Perhaps we should hear the Baptist and his message."

"Perhaps." I now knew there was another journey I must make.

The waters flow and wash us clean.
A rowdy man, a hard and basic man,
A man of simple things and powerful speech.
The waters flow and wash us clean.
A repast of humility, the granary of the sky,
He touches us with sticky fingers and fiery lips.
The waters flow and wash us clean.
He lays us low in deeds heaped upon our heads
Then he proclaims them all un-done.
The waters flow and wash us clean.
He backs away before another,
He bows before the greater hand of love.
The waters flow and wash us clean.
He hands the forgiven off, the heavens torn
And joins the water with the words.
The waters flow and wash us clean.
Oh, Lord, wash us clean and draw us to You.

CHAPTER 4

The Baptist

As I crested a barren and rocky canyon, I wondered why anyone would come here. The Judean desert is a stark contrast to my beloved Galilee. Yet here I met a most interesting group of shepherds. As we stopped to rest in a quiet Judean valley one of the shepherds came to visit with us.

"What brings you to our peaceful Judean hills?"

"We have come here to hear the Baptist speak," I replied as I refreshed myself with the water I carried.

With that the shepherd became excited and revealed to us a most amazing story:

'As you may imagine, we shepherds have a tough, lonely job, but it needs to be done. Those sheep wouldn't last long with all the predators and difficult terrain. They wouldn't even be able to find water to drink or green pastures to feed upon, without us. To be sure, we are a rough bunch, living out in the elements, fighting off predators, and herding often-obstinate sheep over difficult and treacherous places. It takes a very determined and very special person to be a shepherd.

We are not accustomed to a lot of attention. We do our work in the quiet hills around Judea. We actually enjoy the serenity of our job. No noise but the gentle sheep sounds and only the stars and planets lighting the quiet hills. Maybe the shrill howls of meat-hungry wolves might pierce the still night, yet watching sheep sleep the night away, offers little excitement on most nights.

On one particular night, over twenty years ago, our peaceful world was shattered by a being so bright that it took our vision from us and our eyes found it most difficult to adjust from the darkness of the night. We had never experienced the brightness of thousands of blazing torches all focused on us. The lights that we had experienced in the past were only the flickering yellow flames of a campfire. The intense brightness of what we came to believe was the Angel from God made our eyes ache as we tried to look away to ease the pulsing eye strain. We had never known such fear, as the brightness of a thousand sunny days surrounded us.

We wondered why such brightness and grand attention should be focused upon us poor, lowly shepherds and why such important news should come to us. I was a young shepherd in those days, but I had never before or have I since been so completely terrified. Yet the news was a message so important that all the world would be told of it. It was news for all, even for us poor, frightened shepherds. It was the message directly from angels of a baby just-born in the city of David, a Savior, Christ the Lord.

Certainly, we are devout, practicing Jews. We know the Scriptures and their age-old promise of a Messiah. He was the One who would come to save everyone, even lowly shepherds doing their job in the countryside. Now as the Roman Empire ruled our land and subdued us all, we lowly sheep-keepers in the remote hills knew that God was intervening in the world and fulfilling His promise.

The City of David, of course is the little village of Bethlehem. The voice from the light told us the Messiah was there at that very moment. He was just-born, still in the baby clothes of a common birth. We wondered why we were being told directly by God's messengers, we had never felt that we were all that important.

But as we realized the importance of the message we began to actually feel important. Then to really top it off, there was a whole host of these Beings of Light and the brightness was so intense we could scarcely stand. Their voices blasted out to us as they all spoke together. What a chorus, the sound of the largest parade imaginable! We then knew that God was pleased to bring us the peace that overwhelms all generations of the world.

Then just like that they were gone. The world went dark, and we stumbled as our eyes slowly became accustomed to the darkness again. I knew that we must immediately go to Bethlehem to see this for ourselves. Someone said we could not leave the sheep, but I insisted that they would be fine. To appease the others, I appointed the youngest of our group to stay and tend the sheep. They were all bedded down and content for the evening on good pasture. The rest of us left for Bethlehem.

We found the primitive stable, really the bare minimum of protection from the elements. The mother and father were there. In a cattle feed-box they had placed the newborn baby upon a mattress of fine straw. The poor mother, so young and perplexed was speechless when we arrived. When we told her the story of how we knew of the birth, she and her husband only nodded in pure astonishment.

I'm still not sure why God decided to let us know the news first, but if He told us, surely the news must be for all mankind. News like this made us realize that we had to tell others. We aren't a very vocal bunch by nature. We are not given to lengthy conversation, but we had to talk about what we had seen and heard. As we passed through the streets of Bethlehem on our way back to our sheep we told everyone what a wondrous thing had come to pass in their town. I don't know if folks believed the words of a bunch of shepherds telling stories of angels, but we told them to go see for themselves.

Now I must tell you to go hear the Baptist, for he speaks of one much greater than himself. We believe he speaks of the Messiah, the one born in Bethlehem. I have gone to hear and have been baptized by this prophet.'

After listening to the shepherd relate his story, my excitement to hear the Baptist was heightened. It was not hard to find the place where The Baptist preached. I followed the crowds over trails through the dusty terrain. Views of the great dead sea of salt came and went as I approached the place where The Baptist held the crowd of his followers in awe. The ribbon of cloudy water flowed into the valley where it emptied into the Dead Sea. The Jordan River was etched with a strip of green on each shore and there was a level place near the river where a crowd was gathered. The location seemed remote and inhospitable and when I saw him I marveled at his rough and austere appearance. One might even be repulsed at his rugged garments and his appearance as one who has never cut his hair or trimmed his beard.

John looked at his visitors as a shepherd ready to shear them like sheep and then to cast them into the desert terrain to fend off wolves and scorching heat. Yet his every word drew us in and broke our spirits, then immediately lifted us to a new level of understanding.

John had by-passed the Romans and even the Pharisees and Sadducees. He had left behind all respect for the priesthood, for even his father who was a priest was fair game for his preaching.

The Baptist inspired no illusions of temporal victory or the fleeting hope of reclaiming a political or military cleansing of Israel. John spoke of the kingdom of heaven as the ultimate endgame of all humanity. He preached of the Messiah, not as some future hope, but as if he knew the Messiah personally.

"Repent of your sins and show your contrition and your change of heart by being baptized right here, right now in the Jordan River."

Even the leaders of the church came to see him and he gave them the same message that we all received: "Repent and be baptized."

The Baptist cared not whom he offended. His words stung each of us as scorpions. Yet he told us he was not the Messiah, he was only preparing the way for the Messiah. We needed to listen to him, repent, be baptized, and then be ready to follow the Messiah.

Andrew and Simon had journeyed with me to this land that seemed so barren and god-forsaken to us who dwelt by the sea and ate bread and fish. We watched John as he crunched a roasted locust between his teeth, spitting out the wings and then proceeded on with his boisterous preaching. Who could not pay attention?

Andrew turned to me, "I have been baptized by this preacher who speaks with authority and seems to know the Messiah personally and I embraced his message of repentance and also forgiveness."

"Could he possibly know the Messiah; does the Messiah actually walk these hills, is he truly among us?" Simon questioned.

Then I saw him among the followers of John. It was Jesus, my former employee. He immediately saw me and motioned us over to where he stood next to John the Baptist. John turned to Andrew who had previously followed him and had heard his words. Then turning and bowing in humility to Jesus, John said, "Behold the Lamb of God, who takes away the sin of the world! This is He of whom I said, 'After me comes a man who ranks before me, because He was before me.'"

At that moment I was startled as John turned again and abruptly lashed out at a group of Pharisees and Sadducees who had come to hear him: "You brood of vipers! Who warned you to flee from the wrath to come? Bear fruit in keeping with repentance. And do not presume to say to yourselves, 'We have Abraham as our father,' for I tell you, God is able from these stones to raise up children for Abraham. Even now the axe is laid to the root of the trees. Every tree therefore that does not bear good fruit is cut down and thrown into the fire."

"I baptize you with water for repentance, but he who is coming after me is mightier that I, whose sandals I am not worthy to carry. He will baptize you with the Holy Spirit and fire. His winnowing fork is in his hand, and he will clear his threshing floor and gather his wheat into the barn, but the chaff he will burn with unquenchable fire."

"Does that answer your questions, Simon?" I turned to my friend the Zealot and shook my head in wonder.

"The Baptist speaks with a higher authority than even that of the church leaders. He demands repentance of them before he will baptize them. He speaks for the Messiah who will give truly penitent people the Holy Spirit and the unrepentant will be cast into the fire of God's wrath." I was beginning to fully understand the message.

The message seemed to be immediately clear to Simon, "He speaks out against the church leaders who live in luxury and accommodate the Romans. It is the unrepentant nature of our people who have brought subjugation to our land. We need repentance and baptism and we need the Holy Spirit of the Messiah."

"John is indeed a prophet, he brings a message for an unrepentant people." I now knew what Andrew had found.

We listened and watched as many were baptized. I wavered as to my readiness and wondered if my repentance was adequate for me to be baptized. All I knew for sure was that I must return to hear more of this fiery preacher.

Gnarled hands seize the ropes and haul the net.
Dark, suntanned backs to match
The sun-browned hills of Galilee.
Searching daily for the silvery catch
Yet, look beyond the sparkling waves;
The prophets point to One who saves.
Chosen for eternal chores,
They look beyond the rocky shores.

CHAPTER 5

The Fishermen

"**M**oshe, take a day off from building boats and fish with us," Simon approached me early one morning.

"I have a boat to finish," I protested.

"Come help us sail our new craft; maybe you will learn something new and improve your boats," Andrew also chimed in.

So, it was that I sailed with the brothers. I was amazed at how my boat had been outfitted and adapted to its primary use as a fishing boat. Baskets were neatly stacked in the center of the boat. The cast-nets were carefully stowed along the side walls; the weights and lines meticulously organized.

The young day, still lacking sunlight began to brighten on the waters of Galilee. We caught a slight breeze and sailed out to the west. Andrew and Simon stayed in the bow as we sailed. Nearing the opposite shore, Andrew shouted, "There is a school of fish ahead!"

Immediately the sail was lowered and we drifted quietly forward. Both Simon and Andrew readied their cast-nets. The weights and lines were held in perfect organization so the net could be thrown at a moment's notice. I detected ripples in front of us and knew by the dark cloud beneath the surface that a large school of fish lay ahead. As we drifted into the school, both

Andrew and Simon simultaneously threw their nets. The graceful arc of the nets descended in a wide circle, hitting the water at the same time. As the nets sank beneath the surface, the fishermen held the lines that would pull the net closed, encircling the fish and trapping them in the net.

Each fisherman hauled his net in. As each net neared the boat, the other workers and I helped to pull the nets full of fish to the side of the boat.

"Help bring them aboard!" Simon yelled.

As the nets were emptied into the boat, the sorting began. The unclean scale-less bottom-feeders were thrown back and the silvery scaled fish we put into the empty baskets.

Again, and again the nets were thrown and retrieved, each time bringing in a catch of fish.

"Moshe, you bring us great blessing in fish," Andrew turned to me with a satisfied smile.

As the sun began to beat down on the sparkling water, the baskets were filled.

"Let's set sail for Magdala before the heat of the day spoils our catch," Simon, always in control, helped to hoist the sail.

Now the cool lake breeze caressed my face and dried the sweat from my hair.

"God has blessed us with a good catch today," I faced the brothers.

"The tax collector will require forty percent for their share, we will pay our helpers and have enough left over to set out again tomorrow to fish once more," Simon replied.

"But the sea is beautiful and what other life could we want?' Andrew countered.

"At least those of us who live by the sea don't need to chase sheep across the hills, or toil in the field beset with weeds and locusts." I replied.

The boat sailed perfectly and I knew the meticulous care Jesus and I had taken in its construction had paid off with a fine craft.

"What would you change if I built another boat for you?" I asked Simon.

"I would have it sail itself so I could sleep tomorrow morning," Peter replied in a rare moment of humor.

Andrew turned serious, "As I sail upon this water I am reminded of baptism and the message of The Baptist."

"His message haunts me as well," I mussed.

"Maybe we are ready for baptism, Moshe," Simon turned to me..

"Maybe we need to bypass the Romans and all their taxes and focus on the message of our own repentance, and the heavenly end game that awaits us."

"He speaks of the Messiah as a real person, a divine person; one who comes to save us eternally."

"We must go back to the wilderness and find our direction in these days of trial." Andrew turned to me and Simon.

The hull of the boat now began to scrape stones as we approached the shoreline. Thomas and Philip, two new workers who were hired by the two fishing families to help with the catch, ran down to meet us and help bring the fish ashore.

Simon asked Thomas how the sons of Zebedee had faired on the lake.

"John said the fish were scarce where they fished today. I can see by your full baskets that you have proof of a good morning's fishing." Thomas observed the fresh catch.

No flash, no soft-sell words he brings,
From the mouth of one who spits out locust wings
And the words of condemnation in a single voice.
It's our choice to wash in the water of repentance as
The heavens point to another one, the Greater One,
God's own Son.
We are washed we are cleansed, re-born;
By thunder and water on a desert morn.

CHAPTER 6

The Baptist

The trails along the dusty hills of Judea were filled with people who longed to hear the Baptist's message of repentance. Some looked for a solution to the occupation of the land by the Romans. Others felt the need for something beyond the sacrifice at the temple. Perhaps curiosity drove most to hear the powerful preaching of the priest's son John. Most remembered the birth of John and how his father Zechariah had insisted he be named John.

As we followed the tortuous trail through the wilderness we learned much as we met others on the way. We learned that John grew up in the religious practices set down by Zechariah his father. He had studied the scriptures and the words of the prophets. It was revealed to him by God that the true Messiah was coming. The message of the coming Messiah was the message of the prophets, it was a message of repentance and reconciliation.

John was very adamant about baptism. He expected the actual sign of Baptism to guide the people in their spiritual search. He preached repentance as the ultimate bridge to a relationship with God. John gave no one, not even the church leaders a pass on forgiveness and the need for baptism. As we neared the area where John was preaching, we heard the priests and other church leaders comment on John the Baptist.

"He expects us to be baptized, just like the Gentiles who did not grow up in the tradition of the church!" the priests complained.

"Yet he even accepts Roman soldiers and tax collectors to be baptized if they come in repentance."

"Yesterday he condemned Herod for living in sin with his niece who was his brother's wife."

"We will see how long this John is allowed to preach freely in these Judean hills."

And so, we again entered the world of John the Baptist. He was turning the religious world upside down. He did not preach rebellion against the Romans. In fact, he even accepted them, for they too needed forgiveness and he said they could receive it with repentance. He baptized all who came in repentance.

Then I saw an acquaintance in the crowd. We had met in the garden campsite at Gethsemane. It was Simon who had followed the Zealot.

"Simon, you have come to hear the Baptist?"

"Moshe, you leave your tranquil lake for the dry Judean hills?"

"We all came to seek the truth. Meet Simon and Andrew, my fisherman friends."

"Fishing sounds like a restful occupation," Simon the Zealot spoke as he extended his hand to the brothers.

Simon, always attentive to his business said, "You should try it, we are actually looking for some extra help."

"I will give it consideration." Simon the Zealot always seemed honest and sincere as he continued, "my convictions are strong and I have followed the Zealot Barabbas, yet the preaching of John is more powerful and with greater authority than the Zealot even though John doesn't preach rebellion, but repentance and humility."

"It seems he is more in keeping with the message of the prophets and the prophecies of the coming Messiah," Andrew replied to Simon.

We listened to the plaintive voice of John. It was truly a voice of one crying in the wilderness as he lamented our sins. He then moved toward the Jordan River. A large crowd followed The Baptist as he approached a place where the bank was relatively level. Bare and sandaled feet sank into the soft earth of the shore, following as one into the water. People came to him confessing their sins and asking for mercy and the blessings of baptism as a sign of contrition and forgiveness. As they came he immersed them and announced forgiveness.

As we neared the shore, a small group neared the water and then a familiar form walked into the water next to John. "I would be baptized," he said to John. I immediately recognized him as my former employee, Jesus of Nazareth.

"But I should be baptized by you," John protested as he recognized Jesus.

"He is Jesus of Nazareth who worked for you Moshe, again come to hear the Baptist," Simon Peter turned to me.

"Yes," was all I could say.

"Apparently he comes often to hear the words of the Baptist."

Not only did John seem to know Jesus well, but he deferred to him as someone who was greater; a greater prophet. Jesus then spoke to John, and John then took Jesus into the water and baptized him. The next thing that happened startled us all.

"It is a light, like none I have ever seen," Andrew looked startled.

I saw the light and then a dove, and then we all heard the voice. It was larger than the crowd and some thought it to be thunder, yet there was no sign of a storm. The words were clear: "This is my beloved son, with whom I am well pleased." We all heard it and we believed it was God.

After his baptism, the crowd parted and Jesus climbed the hill above and disappeared into the wilderness. I made my way toward the small group of people who had followed Jesus to the river.

"Do any of you know Jesus of Nazareth?" I asked the group in general.

"I am Philip and I have followed and listened to Jesus," one from the group spoke up.

"Of what does he speak?" I asked.

"He speaks of the Kingdom of God and forgiveness. He came to John the Baptist to be baptized."

"Where does he go now?" I asked.

"He said he must go alone to the wilderness to fast and face spiritual trials."

"Where did you meet Jesus?"

"I am a tradesman, as is he."

"I am a tradesman as well, a boat builder named Moshe." I felt an immediate kinship to Philip.

"And you know Jesus?" Philip asked.

"He worked for me in my boat-building business by the Sea of Galilee."

"Yes, I know him to be a skilled carpenter. Now he says he has important work to do for his father. His father, Joseph, is a carpenter, and carpentry is the only work he has known. Yet I followed Jesus because his words have power and authority. John the Baptist speaks of him as one who will supersede him and preach with greater authority."

"How does that fit in with his baptism and his wilderness trials?"

"That is what I am attempting to understand. His father is a humble carpenter working on small jobs for the people near him. I know of no big Roman projects that he has been hired to complete."

"Maybe he has been hired by the Romans to build crosses. I hear they are having trouble getting enough," Simon Peter broke into the conversation.

"What are the words of Jesus?" I asked as I ignored Simon and remembered the conversations I had with Jesus.

"He speaks of the kingdom of God yet he carries no weapons and speaks only of repentance and forgiveness, in a humble and meek manner."

Simon, Andrew, and Simon the Zealot looked on as Philip and I talked.

Finally, Simon spoke to Philip, "What is it that sets this Jesus apart from all the other prophets and rabble-rousers who roam our countryside with various messages."

Philip spoke with quiet, deep intent, "He is one of us."

"Yes, he is a carpenter and works like we do at the labors of his trade, but how does that set him apart?" Simon pressed to get to the real truth.

"You saw it, didn't you? You also heard the voice?" I broke in.

"His words are the words of God," Philip said with great seriousness.

"Andrew, for once you have gone before me, you have been baptized by the Baptist. We too, just as Jesus of Nazareth, should be baptized by John," Simon Peter then started toward the water.

Simon the Zealot, who had been taking it all in finally made a decision that would change his life, "I will also be baptized, for I have seen power today and authority that cannot be matched by the Rebel."

I followed Simon as did Philip, Simon the Zealot, and a number of others who had followed Jesus. We entered the water, filled with repentance and humility. Our lives changed and yet it was only the beginning.

By the solemn crystal flood
Mountain cedar turned to sailing wood.
Galilee's gentle summer draft
Can turn to crush a worthy craft.

CHAPTER 7

The Boat Builder

I had returned to my beloved Sea of Galilee. Boat building had always renewed my spirit, yet some part of me remained at the Jordan River among the dusty hills of the Judean desert. I still heard in my mind the melodious voice of John the Baptist echoing over the flowing waters of the river. The cries of repentance and the dove descending upon Jesus still lived in my memory.

Indeed, we had come back to the Sea of Galilee. I, to my boat building, and Simon and Andrew to fishing. We had shared an experience that changed our lives. We realized our daily need of repentance. It was a transformation in our lives. We knew we needed to take responsibility for our daily actions, and that sacrifices by the priests were only a part of the forgiveness we received.

Simon the Zealot and Philip also followed us to the sea. They were both assured jobs with the fishing families and I also knew I could employ Philip part time helping me in my business. It was about midday on a fine clear day shortly after our return. I saw Philip walking down the shore. He was coming to help me set the ribs on a boat.

"How was the morning's catch?" I asked as he approached.

"We filled nearly all the baskets with keepers. Andrew has taught me to throw the cast net. Once I master the art we will fill the baskets faster. Andrew and Simon seem to put us over the large schools of fish; all we need to do is cast our nets as fast as possible to entrap the fish before they move to a different area."

"It is good to have you here in the afternoons to help with the boat."

"This is really my trade, but the fishing is like play to me; it is relaxing and calms my spirit. Simon is also teaching me to sail the boat and it is very interesting to learn. We ply the breeze and even in a contrary wind we still reach our destination. Perhaps that is how life can turn out."

"Your sailing skills may come in very handy as we complete the boat and we give it a test voyage."

As we measured and pegged the cedar into place, I asked Philip what he thought of Jesus of Nazareth.

"He is unlike any other, he speaks of the Messiah as one who has come. He knows things that seem to be unknown. In the short time that I have known him, he has amazed me with his knowledge of Scripture and his insight into prophecy."

"He worked diligently here when he worked for me," I told Philip.

"We shall see more of him, he speaks highly of the people by the sea and calls this place his home," Philip spoke as we braced another rib on the boat.

"It is good that he should return here. We have all grown fond of him."

Zebedee and his sons John and James were among the best of the fishermen going out from Magdala. They often fished with Simon and Andrew, sailing their boats to the same waters and assisting each other in their quest for good catches.

Philip spoke of the two families and their ambitions in the fishing business.

"Zebedee will be buying another boat soon," he commented.

"He has spoken to me about it," I replied.

"He has proposed an official partnership with Andrew and Simon. If together they can meet a quota and guarantee certain numbers of fish to the broker, they can get a higher price."

"That would help to pay the taxes on the catch," I surmised.

"The processor and exporter to the Empire wants to be able to expand his market and if he is guaranteed the catch from the two families he will be able to control a large market."

"These are good things for a boat-builder such as me." I could see the potential since they were loyal customers of mine.

"It will also mean plenty of work for me and Simon the Zealot."

"We might all prosper a bit, in spite of the Romans."

"The Romans have developed large export markets for our products."

"True, but they exact their pound of flesh from all of us with crushing taxes and license fees."

"The two families will dominate the fishing here in Magdala."

"Sounds like a good reason to get this boat finished," I said, "We will soon be ready for a maiden voyage. Are you ready to sail this boat?"

"Simon has allowed me to sail his boat every day; I think I can handle it."

"We should be ready in two days."

*****

Philip came to help finish the boat. He set the single mast and rigged a sail as I finished shaping and smoothing the oars.

"We will lay down the round, straight logs to make a path to the water for our new boat."

We lifted the boat onto the first log and were able to roll the boat down the gentle slope. We kept placing the logs behind the boat as we pushed it toward the water. With its flat bottom and small draft, it floated in the shallow water near shore.

"We will oar it out until we can catch a breeze," Philip took charge as though he had sailed for years.

Soon we hit a breeze that filled the sail. Philip maneuvered the boat and we set out into the lake. The slight breeze served to move us out a bit further, but mostly the breeze gave relief from the hot, moist afternoon air that hung over the water.

"The boat sails gracefully. I can imagine sailing this boat for Simon or Zebedee, taking it to the great schools of fish," Philip looked up as the wind filled the sail.

We remained parallel to the shore and enjoyed the view of the break-water and the town of Magdala.

As I looked across the great expanse of water to the east, I saw dark foreboding clouds build up over the distant high lands on the eastern shore. A finger of cooler air touched my face as the breeze began to come from the east.

"Philip, has Simon told you of the storms that can blow in from the highlands?"

"We have sailed only on clear days with soft breezes."

"The lake can turn suddenly violent and I feel the cooler air is an ominous sign. Let's turn back toward the shore."

As Philip skillfully turned the boat toward our shore, the zephyr turned into a gusty wind. Soon the waves arose. As we ran toward the shore, waves began to break over the back of the boat.

"We are beginning to swamp," I shouted at Philip.

"We are traveling with the wind and making progress," Philip left the sail in place as we ran before the waves now threatening to fill the boat. Fortunately, we were close to shore and the waves, now much taller than the sides of the boat, raised us up onto the beach.

As the mist blew off the lake, we huddled in the beached boat. As suddenly as the storm had begun, the dark clouds blew over and the wind subsided. We found ourselves beached well above the water line; the large waves having lifted us up onto the dry land.

"We have been blessed and spared. It is good we did not venture too far out on the water," I sighed.

"I have never sailed in such conditions. I felt helpless and at the mercy of the storm," the new sailor seemed shaken by the experience.

"We will need to get help to get the boat back to the water."

"It has never felt so good to be on dry land," Philip confided, "I had no idea this beautiful tranquil lake could be so treacherous."

Wilderness fast,
The strength of a Prophet
To heal the past, He's come
To perfect the future
Not just for some,
Open arms, for all.

CHAPTER 8

Jesus of Nazareth

Sweat dripped from our foreheads. It was a day of heat and moisture coming off the great lake in shimmering waves. Philip and I toiled at shaping the cedar to be used on my next boat. With fine blades we shaped the wood to fit together perfectly.

I looked up to the land above the sea and in a dusty, quivering halo I saw a form emerge. The walk looked familiar, but even at a distance he seemed more hardened, like a well-seasoned cedar. He carried himself with a confident, steady walk. The first time I saw Jesus he appeared less sure, less confident of his path. Now he strode with confident strength. I had seen him last as he climbed the hill into the wilderness of Judea. Now more than a month later he appeared to have gained demeanor, and his lithe form appeared with new purpose, an intense focus. No leisurely stroll by the water, but a strong emergence from the highlands, a trek from his humble, tiny, village of Nazareth. I saw it clearly now, as Philip had pointed out at the river Jordan. He is truly one of us.

"Moshe," said Philip, "you toil by the sea, finding fine crafts in the cedar logs." Jesus, dusty from traveling, approached with a familiar smile and continued Philip's line of thinking, "Cedar can indeed be used for beautiful boats, but also for cruel Roman crosses."

"Come and sit in the shade of my modest shelter," I invited him.

"I will again be staying in Capernaum. I bring a message to the people, our people, the workers, the farmers, the fishermen. They are the kingdom of God. Repentance, forgiveness, and the good news that all can have life. A life beyond the Roman Empire, beyond the daily work. I must carry this message beyond John the Baptist. Here in Galilee are the people of God."

"There are many Gentiles here as well," Philip added.

"They too are the people of God. Life is offered to all who repent and are forgiven."

"Jesus, you are a prophet," I said.

"I am honored to be called a prophet. I must do the work of my heavenly Father."

"You are no longer a worker in wood, the work of your father?"

"I have come to seek and to save the lost."

"Your work is very large," was all I could say.

"You had some time in the wilderness to meditate and ponder Scripture?" Philip asked.

"I am strengthened by the testing of my spirit and I have my Father's power to do the work given to me."

"I sense that the work of which you speak is not the work of Joseph of Nazareth."

"Philip, your sense of understanding is strong. You must follow me and I will teach you to be wise unto eternal salvation."

I looked on as I realized a strong bond developing between Jesus and Philip. Jesus then got up and departed, "I must go to the house of Zebedee and visit James and John."

Philip then turned to me as Jesus strode along the water's edge, "I feel a power and a passion for his words of truth."

"He is indeed the messenger for our times," I agreed.

The next day James and John came to visit. I hoped they were coming to order another boat, but their excitement was focused upon the visit from Jesus and his words of truth and salvation. John beamed with a new light in his demeanor, "Jesus has the words of life; he is the light of all men. He overcomes the darkness brought upon the world by sin. He shines in the darkness and overcomes it. His words changed us."

James said, "He spoke with our family and we have been changed by his words."

I tried to turn the conversation to fishing, "How was the day's catch?"

"All went well," James responded, and then continued, "We hope to see Jesus again this evening, to hear more of what he has to say."

The brothers left as quickly as they had come, anxious to tell others of the prophet they had met. I could feel their excitement, yet I wondered if they needed a new boat.

Philip came over but only worked for a short time. He too was anxious to meet up with Jesus and learn more of His wisdom.

Sleepy village in the hills; olive trees,
Look to Galilee.
One who works in wood,
Mary, Mother of the Nazarenes,
What good,
Could come from there?

CHAPTER 9

Nazareth

It was early on a Friday morning. Simon walked up as I was working in the cool of the day.

"Simon, I thought you'd be out fishing now."

"One of our helpers has taken the boat out this morning. A group of Jesus' followers and I, are going to leave soon to arrive in Nazareth before the Sabbath begins."

"Is there a special occasion in Nazareth?"

"Well, it is Jesus' home town and he will read from the Torah on the Sabbath. We wish to support him as he reads and speaks in his home town. We will leave soon to arrive before the Sabbath begins. Moshe, you should accompany us. You will meet the teacher's family and worship on the Sabbath in the synagogue in Nazareth."

"It is a day's journey, I'm not sure I can take the time."

"You will be taught by the master all the way. You will hear him teach with authority. His words change people's hearts."

"How can I refuse to travel with an old friend, Simon, and my former employee?"

We set out that morning. We felt we would be able to reach the childhood home of Jesus before the Sabbath began at sundown. As we traveled, I could feel the sense of restful conversation. I realized the blessing of the Sabbath. We reached the house of Mary and Joseph before sunset. The meal had been prepared and we ate and talked. Jesus' mother commented, "Tomorrow you will read from the Torah and teach, my son."

"The appointed reading is from the Prophet Isaiah," Joseph commented.

Although I would have enjoyed talk of carpentry and work, we kept away from references to work. In Jesus' house the Sabbath was observed with prayer and meditation.

The next day Jesus stood to read in the synagogue. He read from Isaiah sixty-one, words of prophecy that spoke about the promised Messiah: 'The Spirit of the Lord is upon me, because he has anointed me to proclaim good news to the poor. He has sent me to proclaim liberty to the captives and recovering of sight to the blind, to set at liberty those who are oppressed, to proclaim the year of the Lord's favor.'

I saw in this reading, the teaching of Jesus. As he sat down to speak he said, "Today this scripture has been fulfilled in your hearing."

The people were amazed at the authority with which Jesus spoke. They marveled at the words of Joseph's son. Yet he went on to talk of his ministry in Galilee and the mission to the lost and of the forgiveness he had brought to the diverse people in the Galilean region.

At these words, many began to murmur and complain for they were indeed a community of devout Jews. The church leaders were much offended at these words. His friends and I stood dumbfounded as his own community then drove him from the synagogue and tried to throw him from a cliff near town.

I still don't know how he escaped, but by a miracle he walked through the angry crowd and we all met up and left the area. We certainly traveled farther than we should have according to Jewish law, but we made it back to Galilee by evening.

Jesus told us how it is impossible for a prophet to be accepted in his home town. Undaunted, Jesus went back to his adopted home by the Sea at Capernaum and taught and healed the sick in the synagogue there.

I was told that he cast out demons and healed on the Sabbath in Capernaum and there the people marveled at his authority and the power over unclean spirits. Jesus brought a new fulfillment to the law. People believed it to be good to have compassion and heal people on the Sabbath. Jesus kept the Sabbath and went beyond the law in his compassion for sinners.

Cast nets into the sea,
The catch is great.
Brothers and fathers toil in the breeze,
Cast nets into the sea.
The catch is great, the haul begun.
Nets and words of truth
Deftly woven in the wind and sun,
By the sea, the Prophet has come.

CHAPTER 10

By the Sea

The next day I ventured up the shore toward the north. I wanted to visit with the fishermen as they returned from fishing. They would usually land and sort fish, repair and hang up the nets to dry as one of their helpers would sail down to Magdala to deliver the catch to the fish processors. There the fish were quickly salted and packed for shipment. The breath of the lake teased my nose with the perpetual odor of fish and decomposing water weeds. A gull with no sense of anything but the perpetual hunt for something to eat, climbed the invisible breeze and looked at a world of laboring humans. Peace in a world of change and political confusion held over the sea. My little piece of the shore seemed the same as generations passed through, each exacting its portion of the bounty of the great lake.

I soon came to the place of mooring where Simon and Andrew came to shore. Andrew was throwing a cast net near the shore. My toes curled around the rocks as I struggled for footing watching Andrew cast the great net into the shallows.

"Simon, move over here. I can see the great school," Andrew shouted as he pulled hard to close the net around the fish. The flaxen fibers slid smoothly through the loops and quickly the fish were enclosed in the large circle of the net.

"Pull, Andrew," Simon shouted to him as he struggled to stay balanced on the rocks.

It was a day of calm, rippled water, the sun penetrating the clear surface revealing the schools of the small fish feeding close to shore. Fishing from the shore was an option that day. Casting from the rocky shore was a way to fill in the day, adding to the catch of the morning.

The small fish, the sardines of the common folks were in great abundance that day. They were the salted and broiled fish that mothers sent with children for their lunches. There was always a market for those.

They sorted out the scale-less, unclean, bottom-feeders and cast them back, filling baskets with the silvery sardines.

"We must get these to the salters or the heat of the day will spoil them," Simon, always the older brother, admonished.

"I've been doing this a long time, Brother, I'll get them to the dock."

Simon's cast was long and the net unfurled perfectly. He gave a superior smile as he quickly set the net and closed it. I smiled shaking my head and continued watching. The eternal ritual of brothers in competition unfolded each day.

The sun heated my back and the still air filled my lungs. Heated vegetation and dead fish enhanced the familiar smells and gave me comfort as I gazed out upon the blue lake. Behind me John, the father of Andrew and Simon, repaired nets at the boat, having put in many years throwing nets and pulling fish. I often marveled at the deftness of his fingers as he wound and wove the fibers of flax to keep the nets free of holes and the lines strong and functioning.

As others helped to sort fish, my thoughts turned to current events. "Andrew, what have you heard lately of the Baptist?"

"He points to Jesus as the Anointed One, the Messiah. Right here in Capernaum is the one we are to look to for the words of salvation."

"Do you really think this is the time? Is fulfillment of prophecy at hand?" I asked.

"Moshe, you have heard the Baptist and you have heard Jesus. He is truly a prophet. He champions repentance and urges baptism as the sign of washing and change of heart."

"What do the priests say of him?"

"They listen and stay clear. You know the Romans always fear those who tend to draw followers."

I turned to Simon, changing the subject, "Simon, was it a good day on the lake?"

"Every day is a good day, some are better though. I have already sent our worker to Magdala with a full boat."

"Yet Andrew can't seem to quit fishing," I taunted him.

As Andrew was pulling in what appeared to be dinner, I saw Jesus approach.

He spoke to Andrew and Simon, "Come and follow me and I will teach you to be fishers of men."

I had to ask, "What do you mean by 'fishers of men?'"

"I will teach the good news of life for all who believe, and I will be a blessing to the people who listen and believe."

Andrew and Simon immediately turned their nets and fish over to hired workers, and followed Jesus.

"You have the words of life and salvation," Simon proclaimed as he immediately followed Jesus.

"So, you are Simon the son of John? You shall be called Cephas, which is Peter, for you will be my rock. You are solid in your convictions and if you can lead a fishing boat and find great schools of fish, you will bring many to the truth."

"Moshe, come and hear the words of life," Andrew invited me.

"I must go up and talk to Zebedee," I replied.

"Come with us, we are headed in that direction," Jesus spoke.

We soon came upon Zebedee and his sons as they worked near their boat, fixing nets and repairing baskets.

"James and John, I also need you to come with me to see and learn as I teach in the synagogues," Jesus spoke with authority and the sons of Zebedee immediately followed Jesus.

"Moshe, you are also welcome," Jesus looked to me with a passion I now saw as very special.

"I will come to hear, but I must first speak with Zebedee about a boat."

"Moshe, come and sit and we will talk boats and fish," Zebedee turned the maintenance over to his hired servants.

"It seems as if your business is doing well," I opened as we sat down.

"Indeed, we have great opportunity." Zebedee reclined against the boat, the direct rays of the sun broken by the side of the craft. Zebedee was a rugged man who had lived his life on the water and the leather of his dark face showed a man who had earned everything he had.

"It seems another boat might suit you soon," I spoke directly, without hesitation.

"Perhaps, but other great things are also afoot. We have heard Jesus and his testimony is from God. He speaks as the true Messiah we have waited for," Zebedee, a man of physical strength and also convictions of faith, stretched his intellect far beyond the waters of Galilee.

"I have seen wonders at his baptism by the prophet John."

"My sons are set upon following him as disciples and seeing firsthand what he teaches."

"I would follow him as well, but for the demands of my business."

"Take some time to follow him and find the truth," Zebedee's words spoke to me as the sea sparkled and the gulls seemed to swirl in a celestial veil where Jesus and his followers walked.

His truth spread out upon the waters
"Follow Me" he spoke.
Touched the laboring hearts of all who heard,
His Word.
Called men from every walk, every way.
His truth spread out upon the waters
"Follow Me."
Shouted to the waves and greening hills
To all who heard the Messianic words of old,
Shaping men's hearts and wills.

CHAPTER 11

Disciples

Philip had come to help me that day. I had finally convinced Zebedee he needed another boat. As we worked, Philip talked continuously about the happenings around the Sea of Galilee relating to Jesus. We worked mechanically at our project, but the focus of our conversation was on Jesus and his impact upon all whom he touched with his words and healing.

"I have been with Jesus as he teaches. John the Baptist so specifically pointed to Jesus as the Messiah, the Lamb of God. Jesus has power in his words and also the power of God to not only change people's hearts but to heal their physical infirmities," Philip concentrated on a particularly rough spot on a hull rib he was shaping.

"There He is," I pointed down the shore.

Jesus spoke as the group walked slowly along the shore. As they neared, Jesus came to where we were working, "Moshe, you are building another boat. Soon you will have every fisherman in Galilee floating on your cedar crafts."

"And you will have all the rest of the Galileans following you and listening to your words."

Philip put his tool down and looked with awe at his new-found teacher and mentor. I could see a change in his demeanor and his focus was on Jesus and the group of followers.

Jesus then addressed Philip, "Follow me."

Philip looked at me with a questioning gaze, certainly not one to shirk his work with me, yet I could see a longing in his expression.

"I will be fine, we are on schedule with this boat," I replied to Philip's questioning face. "Maybe you can come by and help me to set the ribs on the keel when I have all the parts made."

With a nod Philip then turned to Jesus, "Teacher, I must go find a friend whom I want you to meet."

"Rest here for a bit in my humble shelter and teach us until Philip returns," I invited Jesus and his followers.

Andrew came over to me, very distraught, "I have heard that John the Baptist has been arrested."

I was shaken by his news for I believed John to be a great prophet.

Jesus then stood up and began to teach, "The time is fulfilled and the kingdom of God is at hand; repent and believe the gospel."

I then remembered the words of John as he spoke of how he must decrease and Jesus must increase. I had wondered how this would happen and now I sadly saw the connecton.

After a while Philip returned with his friend Nathanael. As Nathanael approached, Jesus seemed to know him, "Here is an Israelite in whom there is no deceit."

"How do you know anything about me?" Nathanael questioned.

"You were waiting under a fig tree when Philip came to get you."

Seeing that Jesus was indeed an all-knowing prophet he exclaimed, "Teacher, you are the Son of God! You are the king of Israel!"

Jesus replied, "You will see greater things than these. Truly, truly you will see heaven opened and the angels of God ascending and descending on the Son of Man."

Everyone looked upon Jesus with awe and as he got ready to travel again, all followed him and listened to his every word.

"Moshe, I know you to be a busy and hard-working man. We will see more of you soon." Jesus smiled and strode out into the sunlight.

As Philip and Nathanael followed behind the others I heard Nathanael remark to Philip, "Now I see that indeed a great prophet could come from the sleepy little town of Nazareth."

"In that we can rejoice together." Philip replied.

I had heard his words and seen his power, he truly had the power of God. Yet he was not political. He seemed to agree even with taxation by the Romans. Deep in my heart I wanted him to call down fire and brimstone to destroy the Roman invaders. I didn't realize that his mission was much larger than destroying the Romans. I was drawn to him for I had read the message of the prophets and Jesus was indeed the fulfillment of the prophesies. Out here by the sea we heard and saw him and knew him to be the Messiah. The church leaders seemed not to know him, they had formed a different vision of the Messiah. Yet I knew Jesus to be one of us; come to save us for eternity.

Zebedee's family was totally behind Jesus. Since Jesus healed Simon Peter's mother-in-law, the Zebedee brothers followed Jesus and advocated for his preaching. Zebedee of course continued to prosper with hired help to fish in his boats. Of course, he did order another boat and I was kept busy in my trade. Yet, I was compelled to follow the prophet Jesus whenever I could get away. His preaching in the nearby synagogues and the growing groups of followers drew me as it did the crowds that came to hear.

The wind is off the water,
Change is in the air.
Taxes are collected,
Money hits the table there.
Yet, forgiveness hits the heart,
Wind and words can change the day,
If only the Messiah would come with us to stay.

CHAPTER 12

Levi

I t was to be a very distasteful day as I embarked on a most hated errand. I was headed to the tax collector Levi, to again make my tax payment on a newly-completed boat. The breeze from the lake followed me as I made my way to Capernaum. Roman Centurions bantered with the town's people, passing their boring day and offering just enough authority to let us all know that they were in charge.

As I approached the taxation booth, manned by my regular acquaintance Levi, I saw a line of people there to pay taxes to the Roman occupiers of our land. Some threw their coins down in contempt, while others attempted to cultivate some semblance of a relationship with Levi. The tax collector always kept strict composure and maintained an organized and businesslike demeanor.

Finally, I made my way to the desk of Levi. "How is your day of theft and coercion going," I said in jest.

"Ah, my old friend Moshe; my hope is to charge you double, if I can get away with it," Levi jabbed back at me. I then counted out the exact tax amount. Levi had the records, and we both knew the procedure.

The place of taxation commanded a view of the Sea and also afforded a bit of the sea air that wafted inland. My eyes were drawn to the Sea and there a cyclone of swirling gulls moved along the path headed in our direction. A group of men was engulfed by the birds and soon I recognized the group.

"Moshe," Levi's voice broke my reverie, "do you hate me for my occupation?"

"Levi, we all must make our living," I responded.

"I have heard Jesus of Nazareth teaching in the synagogue. He speaks to the prophets that we all grew up reading in the Torah."

"His words are powerful," I said.

"He speaks of forgiveness and eternal salvation. I think I need that forgiveness."

"So, repentance is what you are saying you feel?"

"Moshe, I feel that my life must change. Maybe it is guilt, but it is also a need for the Messiah that is foretold." Levi's eyes softened from their strict mercenary gaze to a questioning almost pleading stare.

"Jesus speaks with power and authority and his acts of healing are the talk of many people."

As I looked back toward the waters of Galilee, I realized that it was Jesus and his followers who approached as the gulls parted and the Messiah strode toward us.

"Levi, a change in your life approaches," I said as I turned to see the group approach.

Jesus walked up to the table, "Levi, you must follow me."

As though struck by lightning, Levi arose, signaled his assistant to take over the collection, and he walked out to meet Jesus. "Teacher, come to my home and tell me your words of life."

My fisherman friends were among the group who followed Jesus. Andrew asked why I was here and soon realized that I had business with Levi.

"Moshe, take some time and follow us to Levi's house: you will hear the words of a great prophet."

And so, I was drawn once again from business to the essence of life.

Levi lived not far from where he worked. His house was well appointed. Servants took care of the day to day chores of the house. Levi invited us into his house. Jesus sat with Levi at the table and we reclined nearby. Many of Levi's associates also came to the feast that Levi's servants prepared. There was fine food and good wine.

I felt a bit intimidated by all the tax officials surrounding me. I felt them to be illegitimate arms of the Roman Empire. Yet Jesus welcomed them all and His words of repentance and forgiveness touched every one. The close friends of Jesus visited with Levi's associates. John spoke with one named Simeon the tax collector, "Simeon, you collect on our catch each week and it stresses our family income to pay these taxes."

"We do our job John. Just as you fulfill quotas of fish to the Roman exporters, we take the tax required by Caesar."

"Perhaps we all do the bidding of the Romans," John admitted.

"The temptation to take extra beyond our percentage is great, for that we must repent."

"And then change for the better," James added as he listened to the conversation.

Jesus' message was not one of condemnation of sinners, only of repentance and forgiveness.

I could not hate these people for what they did. They did their jobs, much as I built boats.

There were church officials in attendance and they criticized Jesus for even associating with these tax collectors. At these accusations Jesus' voice rose and all stopped talking and listened to him: "Those who are well have no need of a physician, but those who are sick. I have come not to call the righteous, but sinners to repentance." With these words he looked pointedly at the church officials.

I had learned to listen to Jesus' words and examples. He spoke to us in ways we understood and the truth of his sayings cut even the learned scribes and Pharisees to the heart and silenced them into wonder. Who could argue with the truth he taught.

Water into wine, sinners now are blessed,
The wine that flows, is of the very best.
Cana in the hills, hears a mother's pleading call
For her son to lend a hand at the wedding hall.
Repent and change your hearts, a message so divine,
To change the hearts of sinners, like water into wine.

CHAPTER 13

Cana

The invitation came as no surprise to me. My relationship with Zebedee and his family went back a long way. Our families were comprised of fishermen and craftsmen in Galilee. My relationship with Zebedee's family had in fact grown stronger as I grew in the boat-building business. James and John's mother was related to Mary the mother of Jesus. A wedding invitation was a week-long commitment, but I was mostly caught up in my boat-building projects and a journey to Cana, the quiet little village to the west would be a pleasant break. I looked forward to seeing Jesus' mother Mary again at the wedding. I also felt I would enjoy conversation with Joseph, a fellow craftsman in the wood-working trade.

As I traveled to the uplands of the region of Cana and Nazareth, I often turned to view the beloved Sea of Galilee as I ascended to the rolling hills of the highlands west of Galilee. As the fall weather became quite dry the hills now held only meager patches of green where flocks of sheep congregated. Most of the flocks had moved down to lower, greener areas. The tiny village of Cana was tucked between the hills and surrounded by wandering flocks of sheep. As I approached the tiny village, it was not difficult to find the wedding celebration as everyone in the village had come to join in the festivities. The marriage contract had been signed and the bride and groom were both at the groom's house. The celebration was in progress and tomorrow there would be a great feast. As I entered the first room, I was happy to see jars of clean water to cool and relieve my feet of the dust and fatigue of the day's journey.

Jesus and his disciples were already there. I soon found John and he approached me with a smile and open arms, "Moshe, how was your travel from the seaside?"

"A beautiful fall journey among the hills of Galilee," I replied.

"The bride and groom and our relatives are happy to have you join us."

"I hope to see the parents of Jesus," I replied as I was given wine to drink.

"I am certain you will see Joseph; the bride is his niece and he is in the next room."

Andrew approached from the crowd, "Moshe, it is good to see that you were able to leave your boats to attend."

"Perhaps I can make the trip profitable and learn some new wood-working techniques from the father of Jesus."

"I will find him for you. Follow me." Andrew led me to where Joseph sat.

"Joseph, you remember Moshe, the boat builder," Andrew bowed as Joseph turned.

"Joseph, I was privileged to have your son help me in my boat-building business."

"Jesus speaks well of you, Moshe of Magdala."

"His skill reflects well upon his teacher in the carpentry occupation."

"Now he follows a new trade. Rather than shaping wood into useful things he shapes the lives of many people."

"I have heard his words and they are like the rasp and draw knife, shaping men's hearts and souls."

"We knew from the words of angels and dreams from God that Jesus would go far beyond the carpentry business. Shepherds ran from the pastures around Bethlehem to see him. They knew nothing of us yet angels told them to come and see our son where he was born in a stable. You must greet Mary, his mother. She is busily involved in the wedding festivities, but I will introduce you."

As I walked into the room where women were gathered, I could see that the preparations were large and elaborate. Such a large gathering required much food and drink. As we approached Mary, she seemed preoccupied and a bit distracted, "It is good to see you, Moshe. Jesus much enjoyed working with you."

"He was a great help."

"Now I must find him to help me procure additional wine for the celebration," Mary looked nervously around the room.

I turned to Joseph, "She seems as dedicated and industrious as her son."

"She gets much done," Joseph replied with a tense smile. "When anyone around Nazareth needs help with any project, they just ask Mary and she plans and gets it organized."

Mary entered the adjacent room, the one where I had first entered. I saw then that Jesus was there. Andrew noticed Jesus about the same time as I. "Come and greet Jesus."

As we approached we heard Mary tell Jesus that the guests were running out of wine. I wondered if someone had forgotten to bring enough for the day. Jesus seemed calm and his demeanor seemed to reassure his mother. She instructed the servants to follow Jesus' instructions. Jesus then instructed the servants to fill the stone jars that hold the water for washing.

We heard him say then, "Now draw some out and serve it to the master of the feast." With that done he turned to us, greeted me and said we too should take from the jars and taste.

Andrew exclaimed, "It is fine wine!"

I realized it was a miracle as I tasted the wine that a moment before was water for purification. "Teacher, you are indeed the Messiah. Your powers are those of God!"

"Wine is for the body, yet repentance and forgiveness are for the soul and such things are eternal," Jesus' soft-spoken words cut to my heart.

Throughout the celebration the quality of wine from water was recognized. I now knew this Jesus to be the holy one of God; our deliverer.

The disciples of Jesus whispered in awe as they realized that not only Jesus' words were powerful, but his power extended far beyond words.

Later in the day I visited with Simon the Zealot and asked him, "Do you still listen to the rebel and his message?"

"I have come to realize that the message of Jesus goes far beyond the message of Barabbas. Jesus delivers real attainable solutions to the dilemmas of God's people."

I enjoyed the wedding festivities and was able to converse with Joseph about the latest workings of our trade. Yet as he spoke, I sensed a growing belief in Joseph that his son was to accomplish far greater things than the shaping and fashioning of wood.

After the wedding celebration Jesus and his followers returned to Capernaum. I traveled with the group, back to the seaside. Jesus taught us as we walked and I embraced my faith in God in a new way.

Cast your nets upon the sea,
Follow me.
What are fish, but to a fisherman?
What are nets upon the sea?
Where to cast, the secret known,
Only by thee.
Cast your nets upon the sea,
Follow me.
Cast my words upon the throng.

CHAPTER 14

By the Sea

I toiled in the cool of the early morning. Andrew and Simon Peter also were out in their boat casting nets, not far from shore. The sun had begun to rise and cast its reflection upon the water. As I watched for a moment as the brothers cast their nets, I realized that even they were also much like me. They too seemed drawn back to the Sea of Galilee. It was hard for them as it was for me to totally abandon life near the water. Even as I was working in the cool breath of the new day and shaping the ribs of another boat, I noticed that the nets of the fishermen were coming up empty as they retrieved them. It seemed to be an unusual day for these crafty fishermen.

Down the shore I again saw the swirling cloud of gulls and then I noticed a figure on the beach working over something. Perhaps he was cleaning fish to prepare them for broiling. As the gulls dipped and landed around him he stood up and began walking toward me. The gulls were indeed feasting on the fish cleanings, but they then followed the figure and I immediately realized it was Jesus. As he came near to me the gulls dispersed, "Moshe, such a fine morning to build a boat!"

I walked to the water's edge and greeted him, "You must be planning fish for breakfast."

He carried a basket of fish he had cleaned.

He turned out to Andrew and Simon, speaking loudly, "Go out another sixty cubits and cast there."

Peter said, "We've fished since early morning and have nothing to show for it."

Yet, I noticed they followed Jesus' directions and moved out. They each threw their net and as the nets closed I saw immediately the lines tightened and they both heaved mightily on their nets.

"Jesus, you seem to know the fishing business better than even those two professionals."

As they beached their boat, I saw that all the baskets were overflowing with fish.

Andrew looked at Jesus in awe, "Master."

Without another word, Jesus turned to a pile of driftwood and prepared a fire, "Come, we will broil fish for breakfast. Moshe, join us."

"You are the master teacher, yet you serve us?" I replied.

"I came to seek and to save the lost. There are so many Gentiles near Galilee and they come and hear and are saved. They too are my people. The Messiah comes for all. The church leaders question my words. They try to diminish my message. Here by the sea the people hunger for the words of life and embrace my teachings."

Simon interrupted, "Lord, your signs are clearer each day. Even the fish heard your commands."

"Come and eat," Jesus looked at Simon. "Soon you will seek much more important things than fish. You will focus fulltime on the message of salvation."

Andrew picked a fish from the fire, "But fish are very important."

Jesus pulled the blackened skin from a once-silver fish and smiled knowingly at the fishermen. I wondered if these fishermen would ever completely leave their beloved sea. I looked across the water, my solace and home, and wondered what new changes and revelations were ahead.

Abruptly I stood up, "I must finish the frame of the boat I am working on."

As I walked back to my project, I saw one of the family workers come to get the catch of fish and Jesus began to teach Peter and Andrew.

Prayer on a mountaintop, earnestly outpoured,
A prayer to seek the wisdom of our eternal Lord.
The answer to our teacher's prayer, A ragged group awaited there.
Each one a perfect piece of the master's plan unfurled,
A rugged group of common folks sent out to change the world.

CHAPTER 15

The Apostles

After Jesus came into my life, I began to take more vacations, more breaks from my beloved daily occupation. It happened on a gentle morning as I worked, that Andrew walked up the shore and stopped to talk.

"Moshe, you need a break from working."

"But I like what I do and I have much of it to do."

"Today is your day to take a walk with us."

"Why would I do that?"

"Jesus is about to make some important decisions and you should come to support him."

"What decisions?" I asked as I put down a draw knife to give better attention to Andrew.

"He headed up into the highlands above the lake last night to pray earnestly. He needs a break from preaching and healing the sick to talk to the Heavenly Father. Jesus has many devoted followers, and yet he needs a core group to be apostles, to help him in his teaching and preaching. The harvest of souls is indeed great and full-time help is needed."

"Has he not returned?"

"Sometimes he prays earnestly for many hours. We are going to head up to the mountain to meet him."

"Andrew, would you want to commit full time service to his ministry?"

"If he considers me worthy, I am willing. Surely Peter will be considered. He is such a leader and organizer, he would truly embrace the work of Jesus."

I dropped my tools and we headed north and met up with Peter, John, and James along with dozens of other followers of Jesus.

As we climbed to the higher elevations, the breeze sang to us and I listened to the excited conversation as the group of followers discussed who might be chosen to be Jesus' closest assistants. I still can hear the excited words as the group recited Jesus' words and re-told his parables. I could only listen and learn. I knew as never before what a special group of people I traveled with. I felt a part of them yet I also felt inadequate. I didn't think I could ever be so devout and so ready to give up all of my life to follow the master to whom these men were all so fully committed. I knew many of these fellow believers and knew how they would fit in as great leaders of an exciting movement.

I saw him moving down the mountainside in a place where there was no established trail. He had appeared from a little glade, a hollow where few people explored and a flock of sparrows flew in a flashing veil around him.

Our group of followers numbered about thirty-five men. We waited and visited quietly as Jesus made his way down the slope. There seemed to be a sense of excitement and relief as Jesus descended from the mountain. We all knew he had made a decision and everyone was ready to follow his decision. We knew that God's blessing was upon this group and the decision our Lord had made.

As he arrived in the midst of our group he greeted each of the twelve chosen leaders with a kiss and words of love and encouragement.

"Simon Peter, you are indeed a rock and a leader among men. Words come easily for you. Words spoken wrongly are hard to recall. Yet forgiveness is always yours. Your wife is also your great support. You must lead the circumcised Jews to faith and forgiveness."

"Andrew, your passion for my words is your greatest strength. By your witness your brother Simon came to follow me and now you will lead in your own quiet yet powerful way."

"Brothers James and John, you are indeed sons of thunder. James, your wisdom of the world, and John your love for me and my words, will empower you. James I can only promise that the world will reject you but eternal victory is yours. John, I love you as a brother and your mastery of my words will be for all time."

"Phillip, you are one of my own; an industrious laborer, and now you will work to bring my words of salvation to many, just as you brought my words immediately to your brother Nathanael, witnessing that I had come as the one foretold by the prophets."

"Nathanael, in your hometown I turned water into wine and so you too will turn hearts of those in faraway places to my words of Life. You recognized me even when others in my hometown of Nazareth rejected me. A plain and simple small-town boy, you will travel far and accomplish great things."

I then saw Jesus turn to Levi, known as Matthew the tax collector. I was amazed as Jesus greeted him with a kiss and embraced him as an apostle. I was moved with forgiveness of any ill thoughts I may have had for the man. "Matthew, despised for your occupation, yet forgiven and saved, you will use your great talent with words to help my words to become eternal. You will travel far." Now I knew Jesus to be the greatest transformer of men's hearts, and so he transformed me.

Next Jesus addressed Thomas, "Thomas you will keep your fellow apostles honest, always questioning and seeking the truth. Your loyalty, even unto death will uphold believers."

I was surprised as Jesus embraced James the son of Alphaeus. I knew little of him, yet someone who was little known was loved and respected by Jesus. "James son of Alphaeus, you will be great in my kingdom and will lead to the salvation of many." James seemed surprised by the honor of being an apostle, yet he took the responsibility seriously. So, it was that Jesus changed people.

Certainly, it was no surprise to me when Jesus greeted Simon the Zealot as an apostle. I knew Simon to be passionate and he turned all his passion and loyalty to Jesus.

"Simon, I welcome your fierce passion and loyalty. Now you have embraced the true way to freedom and salvation."

Jesus then turned to Judas also known as Thaddaeus, "I have revealed myself to you because you love me and so it will be for all who love me. You will help instill that love in many."

Judas Iscariot stood close to me, yet I knew little about him except that he was not from Galilee, not a man of the water or the land. Jesus turned and greeted him with a kiss. "Judas, you too will follow me and I greet you with a kiss. Then with a quiet voice I could just barely hear, Jesus said, "A kiss can also betray." Jesus looked at him intently, a smile of compassion lit his face. I wondered at those words of Jesus, not knowing what he meant.

The inner group of twelve walked close to Jesus as we slowly returned from the mountain. As we walked and talked, Jesus dropped back to where I was following. "Moshe," he said, "you too will follow me." The sea is not your only need.

"I must work the wood, for boats are my great love."

"Indeed, wood will save you, but not the wood of boats."

I wondered at his words. In a couple of years those words would come back to me and the truth of those words would indeed set me free.

Blessed are they,
In words that echo on the water.
Blessed are they,
In words from the Father.
Words that ring across the hills,
Touch shepherds and farmers,
Sing to all the humble hearts.
Blessed are they
Who fish, and toil in wood,
Humble, in repentant mood,
Sing words to those who know
They are the forgiven;
Pride laid low.

CHAPTER 16

The Mount

To be back on the tranquil shore of Galilee, was my comfort. Deep in my heart, I was also happy that Jesus and his close followers were back as well.

I worked on a boat, not rushed, as it was a boat that was yet un-sold, but I knew that someone would need it. This boat was a labor of love, it was fastened with the greatest precision and its boards were smoothed with the greatest of care. It felt so good to be back by my beloved sea waking to the sound of the gulls as they swirled in flashing clouds above the water.

Happy was I also to have my friends and their teacher Jesus, back in Galilee. The reports of those who passed on the shore each day were of great wonders of healing and compassion from Jesus. I heard how he taught in the synagogues around Galilee and everyone spoke of how they wanted to see and hear this great prophet. Sometimes I longed to follow the crowds to where he taught and preached.

Then one morning as my boat was just complete I saw Philip walking by himself. He came to my shelter and as he arrived I greeted him, "Philip, you're just in time to help me move this fine boat to the water."

"Moshe, it is the crown of all your projects," He stood with hands on his hips and gazed at the boat. He then ran his hands lovingly along the sides and inspected the smooth seats and perfect bins in which to place the fish baskets.

"The mast is true and perfect and smooth," he stared up the tapering pole.

"I can help you but I came to tell you of an event that you might want to attend. I and the other eleven of Jesus' closest followers are out telling all who will listen that Jesus will have a special teaching session tomorrow."

"Where will this teaching take place?" I asked as I readied some rollers to help launch the new craft.

"On the great mount just west of here. He will sit up on the highest rise and that will allow room for great crowds to come and listen."

"Why such a special occasion?"

"Great crowds press to hear him. As you know, he speaks with great authority. Matthew records much of what he says, and suggested such an event would be greatly loved and widely attended."

"My old friend Levi; I knew he had greater things to accomplish than collecting taxes."

"Moshe, come to hear. I will save you a place close to the great teacher." After helping me move my boat, Philip hurried on to alert all those he met, to the great event.

I rose early the next day to go to hear the teacher. As I ascended the heights above the sea, I was amazed at the lines of people coming on all the trails heading to the great mount. The mount was a very popular place for various groups to meet and teachers to speak to large groups of people. As I saw the people coming together I heard them speaking and sensed an excitement that had not been evident as long as I could remember. I heard people speak in many different dialects. There were fishermen, farmers, craftsmen, government workers, scribes, Pharisees, Roman soldiers, men, women, and children.

It was as if a great festival was to be celebrated. Certainly, there were devout Jews, but also many Gentiles from many regions, all come to hear the message of repentance, forgiveness, and Jesus' unique and comforting message for all people.

Some of course came to criticize his teaching, but most had seen and heard his message and miracles and wanted to see and hear more. As the crowd assembled below, I saw Jesus and his disciples gather up on the highest point.

As I neared, Philip waved at me and I weaved my way between the crowds of people to reach the place where Jesus would speak. I sat near his closest followers and I felt unworthy to be with such a special group.

As Jesus began to teach, the first words drew me to the gaze of Simon the Zealot. Jesus taught how those who would be blessed were indeed those who were meek and were peacemakers. As Simon the Zealot looked at me he nodded and I knew he understood the true revolution and its meaning. Jesus and his followers were the rebels who would triumph eternally. These meek and forgiving followers would be the salt of the earth and they were now commissioned to let the light of Jesus' words be seen everywhere.

Jesus is the fulfillment of the Scripture that we grew up with. The laws are God's Laws but can now be accomplished through the words and teaching of the Messiah. Through Jesus we can now have a higher interpretation of the law. Only through his message of repentance and forgiveness can we keep to the law.

The law according to Jesus is much different. He tells us to love our enemies and assures us that his forgiveness is free to all who come to him in faith. He then spoke to the crowd a simple prayer, a prayer for all, to be spoken not with outward displays, but quietly and in silent words to God.

In every word Jesus spoke of humility and meekness. He assured everyone that they need not be anxious about bodily needs and as he always seemed to do, he referred to those things we common folks all understood. We, like the birds of the air need not worry about everyday needs, for God will take care of his people eternally.

Judging others is not our duty. We are called to speak the words of truth as Jesus spoke them. We are to love and do to others the same as we want done to us. Jesus taught all who follow him to live a life of forgiveness. We must build our life on the rock of his teaching and nothing can destroy our life, for his word is the word of life.

Now I saw even more deeply why he was here among the common folks who came to him. I looked at his twelve closest disciples and now I knew why they were his closest friends. He preached a plain and simple message, so all-encompassing that it was not understood by the high-minded Pharisees. He was here for all of us who knew we needed a Messiah. He taught us plainly and I saw the light of understanding embrace all who heard his words. Just as his words were spoken in compassion, I saw his compassion for all. He healed with his divine power and I saw lepers cleansed, blind given sight, and all manner of infirmities healed. I followed him back to the sea.

Be still, winds,
He stands before the gale,
Without him, can we sail?
Hills beyond,
Pale and green.
Bedeviled swine.
Sent to save the Gadarenes.

CHAPTER 17

The Sea

I descended from the mountain, surrounded by masses of people. I saw Jesus, swarmed by a swirling wall of humanity. Some came to question, some to applaud his teaching. Yet he stopped and even after exhausting hours of teaching, he paused as those with infirmities came to him for help. The accounts of his healing had drawn the masses and as each leper, each frail and broken person approached him, I saw his drawn and tired face turn in loving compassion as he healed or comforted all who came to him.

I stopped as we finally neared the consoling quiet of the calming sea.

"Teacher, I will follow you wherever you go," a scribe approached him.

With sagging and exhausted eyes, he turned to the man, "Foxes have holes, and birds of the air have nests, but the son of man has nowhere to lay his head."

I then knew what sacrifice was required to follow Jesus. I thought I might be able to follow him, but as the consoling waters spread before me, I did not know how I could follow him, as my boats called to me.

It was then I remembered my newest boat on the shore not far away, "Jesus, the crowds have worn you out, come lay your head down in my boat. I and Philip and Andrew will take you across to the west side. Perhaps there you will find rest."

Jesus only smiled and followed me to the boat. As we reached the boat, the crowds seemed to know that Jesus must depart.

"I will rest as we sail, but even across in the Gentile lands of the Gadarenes, there are many who long to hear the words of salvation."

"Rest as we sail; the others will follow in Peter's boat."

Even though I had no courage to follow, I needed to offer my boat and the calming embrace of the waters of Galilee. As we sailed to the west, I soon knew that the tranquility I sought would not persist. The clouds built across the opposite shore and dived to the water, bringing with them a tempest even greater that any I had seen in my years living by Galilee. The waves built to great heights and my friends and I knew that even my new and sturdy boat could not withstand their force.

Jesus slept the peaceful sleep of exhaustion, yet we feared for our lives as the waves came over the sides of the boat.

"Lord, only you can save us," Andrew yelled and awakened Jesus. He rose and in perfect steadiness stood and faced the fierce wind. His hair blew straight back and his garments pressed to his body as the teacher looked straight into the wind, raised his arm and with calm authority told the wind to stop.

As if frozen and thawed, the waves turned into a perfectly calm sea.

"After all you have seen and heard, you still have fear. Your faith must become stronger."

I turned to Philip, "He is no ordinary man. Even the winds and the sea obey him."

Philip nodded in awe, "He is truly the son of God."

We reached the opposite shore in quiet reverence.

Finally, as we neared the shore Andrew spoke, "Up beyond the steep bluffs is Gadara."

I then heard a sound that gave me peace and security as the wood of my boat bumped and grated upon the rocks near shore. I jumped out along with Philip into the shallow water and we pulled the boat up to the shore.

Jesus awoke, stood, and stretched his arms as he gazed up the steep bank to the hills beyond.

"Here is a place of quiet and a restful land," I said as the other boat followed us to shore.

I had no more than spoken those words than I heard a loud wailing cry up in the hills. The violent voice echoed through the cuts and canyons that led to the shore from the highlands. Then I saw him, bleeding and cursing. The stones rolled down the steep bank as he came toward us, throwing stones and all the while his harsh voice echoed over the hills. He put great fear into me and I feared we would need to retreat to the boats.

Jesus stepped up toward the raging man and the man stopped, and cried out, "What have you to do with us, Son of God?"

At this I marveled for the man seemed to know Jesus.

"He is possessed by demons," Peter shouted out. And then the man calmed a bit and seemed to beg Jesus, "Don't send us away, let us remain here in the land of these who do not know God."

I knew that the demons spoke through the man, and as I glanced to the high hill I saw a herd of swine rooting and feeding on a hillside. The man then spoke as he looked to the hill. "Send us into the herd of swine."

Jesus spoke one word, a word that rang above the chaos of the demon-possessed man, "Go!"

Immediately I saw the herd of swine begin to squeal and rampage in senseless disorganization. Then suddenly one large boar headed down the steep slope and all two-thousand of the herd raced behind him. They were all headed in unstoppable hast toward the water below. As they hit the water in a dizzy frenzy they all disappeared in a swirling mass and the water covered them.

The man sat at Jesus' feet, calm and serene.

"Lord you have driven the demons from the man!" I spoke, as no one else could voice what they had seen.

The herdsmen who witnessed the incident begged us to leave, that no more destruction would come to them or their town of Gadara.

We found an extra garment for the man who now spoke calmly.

"I wish to stay with you," the man spoke to Jesus.

Jesus then replied, "Go home to your friends and tell them how much the Lord has done for you, and how he has had mercy on you."

The man is known to have gone to Gadara and all over the Decapolis proclaiming what Jesus had done for him. Even here everyone marveled at the authority of Jesus and the word spread through this incident.

Quiet hills on lakeshore views,
From distant towns to hear his news.
Healed and fed they walked, amazed,
And we will learn to walk on water,
Learn to follow, heavenly dazed.

CHAPTER 18

Solace by the Sea

S imon and James approached me as I worked, "We have news that is not good news."

I dropped my tool and turned to Simon, "What news do you bring?"

"The Baptist has been executed by Herod," James stared at the water as he related the news.

"His message was so powerful," I was stunned.

"We brought the news to Jesus and he was clearly saddened."

The two departed quickly, headed up the shore to their families. I sat down to think about the sad news, for The Baptist had deeply influenced me; not to mention his having baptized me, and brought me to repentance.

I closed my eyes and the pungent smell of wood shavings calmed me with their wonderful familiarity. As I sat with my back to the sea, a cool breeze drying the sweat from my neck, I caught a glimpse of a flock of sparrows as they swirled in the wind. There I saw the familiar form of Jesus. Silhouetted in the chirping, swirling cloud of wings and tail feathers, he headed straight toward me.

"Jesus, what a blessing to see you," I stood as he entered my shelter.

"Moshe, you are also blessed among men," he greeted me with a kiss.

"I am saddened to hear about the Baptist."

"The news has given me much sorrow, I would like a brief respite from the crowds."

"There is a desolate place across the lake, south of Bethsaida. I could take you there in my boat," I offered thinking of Jesus' need to rest and be relieved of the crowds that followed him each day.

"Moshe, what a blessing. Galilee is calm and restful today, a perfect day to sail. My disciples are headed up the shore to their families and will meet us later, for they know the place."

Jesus rested as we sailed and as we reached the shore stepped out onto a deserted beach, "I know the crowds will come as my disciples come to this place. Stay and listen and visit with those who hear me."

Although we had crossed to a place known for its desolate solitude, the people began to arrive, knowing that Jesus would be here. I was amazed at the numbers of people and how they came with faith that they and their friends would be healed of all types of infirmities.

I saw a weary Jesus turn to the crowds and the compassion on his face melted to a newly invigorated demeanor as the people sought just to be near him or to touch his garment. I saw the healing and the acceptance of his teaching.

There were at least five thousand people and as the day wore on all of Jesus' chosen twelve disciples arrived. They helped bring the people to Jesus.

As the day waned into late afternoon Peter came to Jesus, "These people need to go to the towns and buy some food and leave you to take a break from the crowds."

"Peter, they don't need to leave, you can give them something to eat."

"We have only two small fish and five loaves of bread. There are five thousand people to feed."

Jesus asked them to bring what they had and to have the people sit down on the grass. Jesus then took the loaves and fish, looked up to heaven and blessed the food. He then began to break the bread and fish into pieces, giving the food to the disciples to distribute to the multitude.

As Jesus broke the bread and the disciples distributed the food, all of the thousands of people had food to eat. The leftover food filled twelve baskets. All I could do was marvel at the power of Jesus to provide for the peoples' needs.

I turned to Jesus, "Lord, heal me of my lack of faith and my obsession with serving only my own needs."

"Moshe, you will follow me."

At this I wondered how it could happen as I embarked to sail home.

Peter and some of the disciples sailed with me as some stayed to help Jesus dismiss the crowds to their homes.

"Jesus will take time to pray and rest. He will meet us back on the western shore," Peter began to unfurl the sail.

We sailed against a strong wind that night. By three in the morning we were still tacking against the wind, trying to make progress and reach our home shore of the great lake.

We all saw it at the same time and I remember the hairs standing up on the back of my neck. It was a sight I had never seen before in all my years on the Sea of Galilee. It was the form of a man and we thought it was ghost-like in appearance. Yet as it approached walking upon the waves we recognized it as Jesus as he spoke, "Take heart; it is I. Do not be afraid."

Peter saw that it was Jesus and of course Peter immediately believed that if Jesus could walk on the water, then he too could do it.

Jesus commanded Peter, "Come." And I watched him step out of the boat and onto the surface of the sea. Peter walked on the water until he was near Jesus. As Peter looked around at the treacherous waves, he began to sink. Jesus reached out to him, "Why did you doubt?"

As they entered the boat the wind ceased. I looked at Jesus and he gave me a compassionate smile.

"Moshe, you will follow."

"You are truly God, but how can I follow?"

"I have revealed to you and you have seen. Many will follow who have not seen. They have only heard, and you must tell them."

He has control of the very sea that gives me solace yet how could I follow him?

Authority of Messiah,
Traditions on the run.
Messiah's words undefiled,
Mighty cedars touch the sun.
Forested hills give up their bounty
Words can save us or defy us,
We must choose whom to follow
Cedars float or crucify us.

CHAPTER 19

Synagogue to Forest

I did not follow him as they did; the twelve who had forsaken all to be with him. Yet I did follow, at times, as he said I would. But then the water and boats would lure me back to my safe place on Galilee. The more I heard him speak with such wisdom and authority, the more I longed to hear him, the more I came to love him.

"Moshe, come to hear him. The Jewish leaders from Jerusalem have come to hear him. His fame spreads to all corners of our land." Andrew came by and entreated me.

"Where is he now?" I put down my tools and tied my sandals.

"He has just spent time at Gennesaret, very close to here. He has been healing many people; all those that came just touched his sleeves and in faith they were healed. Now I expect him to go up to Capernaum and speak with the church leaders from Jerusalem."

"I will come to hear him. Some of the Scribes and Pharisees seem to resent his teaching."

"They don't recognize him for who he is," Andrew said.

It was a busy day in Magdala as we passed through the busy seaside market and headed up toward Capernaum. The buzzing flies and the smell of fish in the air turned our senses. The small waves glittered like diamonds as we walked rapidly north along the water.

We arrived at the synagogue as the Pharisees and scribes crowded around Jesus. I saw Simon and the other apostles were also in the circle of people gathered to hear Jesus.

The Pharisees and scribes seemed set upon criticizing Jesus and his doctrine of practical love and compassion. I heard them say that not washing hands before eating was a serious breaking of the traditions set down by the church leaders. At this I wondered how simple people of the land and water could keep all of these rules as they set about the common work that was before them.

Jesus answered their complaints with a question to them, "Why do you break the commandments of God for the sake of your traditions?" He said God commanded us to honor our fathers and mothers, yet the church leaders invented reasons to not honor and care for parents.

Jesus then so eloquently quoted scripture, where Isaiah said, 'This people honors me with their lips, but their heart is far from me; in vain do they worship me, teaching as doctrines the commandments of men.'

Then Jesus spoke to us, his people, "Hear and understand: it is not what goes into the mouth that defiles a person, but what comes out of the mouth; this defiles a person." Thus, Jesus contradicted the church leaders and their petty rules on cleanliness. I could see that the disciples were astonished and they saw that the Pharisees were much offended when they heard what Jesus said.

Jesus then turned to a group of us and said, "Every plant that my heavenly Father has not planted will be rooted up. Let them alone; they are blind guides. And if the blind lead the blind both will fall into a pit."

Peter needed more clarification of what Jesus was saying, "Explain the parable to us."

Jesus replied, "Do you not see that whatever goes into the mouth passes into the stomach and is expelled? But what comes out of the mouth proceeds from the heart and this defiles a person."

All that Jesus taught made sense to me. Here was indeed a prophet with a new and forthright understanding. Certainly, he was one of us.

Philip came to me then, "We are going to follow Jesus to the north. He wishes to find some peace and quiet in the district of Tyre and Sidon." Jesus was headed to the north where the wood for my boats originated. I had traveled there before searching out the perfect cedar wood for my boats.

"I will take the time to follow to the north. Two days' travel will bring us to the land where my boats originate." I spoke with enthusiasm for an interesting sojourn.

"Perhaps the Lord knows you need to travel here as well." Andrew welcomed me to the traveling group of disciples.

As we entered the district near Tyre and Sidon a Canaanite women who had apparently heard of Jesus' great power over demons came and asked Jesus to help her daughter who was oppressed by a demon. Many in our group said he should send this foreigner away. Some still felt his power was only for the Jews, yet he helped the woman and praised her faith in him. The daughter was healed instantly. We witnessed the change in her. Once again it was evident that anyone from any ethnic background who had faith was welcomed by Jesus.

"You see now Moshe, why the Pharisees and scribes so despise Jesus? He makes no distinction between Jews and Gentiles. His forgiveness and saving message are for all people," Simon the Zealot, caught up to me as we traveled on. As we traveled up into the highlands the day cooled and we felt the moist air of evening. The mellow weather reminded me of an evening by Galilee. Perhaps this is why the wood from this area seemed so natural when shaped into my boats.

We stopped for an evening at a mountain glade among beautiful cedar trees. Many travelers camped at this place. As we sat by a fire warming ourselves, I met a fellow craftsman who was there to purchase wood for his projects.

"I am Simon from Cyrene. I have come all this distance to purchase wood from these great cedars." As the man from Cyrene stood up to greet me, he towered over me. His shoulders and arms were as of steel. Indeed, he was a man who could build large, heavy projects.

"I am Moshe and I too use the fine cedar wood to build my boats that ply the Sea of Galilee."

"It is always good to meet a fellow tradesman."

"I have come here as part of a group, following Jesus of Nazareth, please sit by our fire."

A smile crossed Simon's face, "I have heard of Jesus and his teaching, I am of the Jewish faith. Jesus has achieved some fame and also some concern among the Jewish church leaders."

"How is it that you know of the controversies of the Jewish faith?"

"Since I too am a Jew, I travel each year to Jerusalem to celebrate the Passover."

"Come my friend, hear the words of Jesus and his teachings. As a Jew you believe in the coming Messiah. Jesus is the promised Messiah."

Simon of Cyrene listened to the authoritative teaching of Jesus and I could tell he was touched by the words.

"Jesus, I will hear more of you. My faith and work take me often to Israel. I may wish to be baptized," Simon spoke late in the night, after hearing Jesus speak his words of faith and repentance.

The next morning as we began to get ready to return to Galilee, I saw Simon of Cyrene for a short conversation.

"If you get to Galilee, stop to see me. I am on the shore by Magdala. Everyone there knows me."

"I will find you."

"Before we depart I must ask you Simon, what type of wood products do you build?"

"Right now, I have a large contract with the Romans to build crosses."

"Does it not disturb you that so many of our fellow country-men die on those crosses?"

"Moshe, it is a living in these stressful times."

"Maybe you could do better."

"Yes, and perhaps you Moshe, could also do better."

"Maybe," was all I could say as I got up to follow back to my little world in Galilee.

Sent out with just the Word
To preach and heal and cure.
Faces lit by God's own Spirit,
Swirling birds, white and pure.
Sent out with just the Word,
Messiah's promise of power and signs
Changing hearts and saving souls,
A message that eternally binds.

CHAPTER 20

Sending from the Sea

For me it began as a typical day. I worked early, as the sun spread its golden wonder upon the water. I looked west across the water as schools of fish broke the surface and the beginning of a breeze touched the lake.

A sight that was at the same time familiar and unfamiliar occurred as I saw my fishermen friends, Peter, Andrew, John, and James walking down the shore from the north. Familiar friends, yet the thought of them walking the shore on such a fine morning, and without nets or lines was most unfamiliar.

They came to a place where they often met Jesus and the others. Soon more familiar faces arrived, some from the south, others from the west. I saw them all drawn to the place of meeting. I recognized Philip, my craftsman associate and Bartholomew, Thomas and my old friend Levi, James and Thaddaeus, Simon my rebel companion, and Judas Iscariot. All of them dressed for a day, no lunch, no extra clothing or sandals.

Then I saw the cloud of swirling shore birds. Their wings flashed in the early sunlight and the sound of a whirlwind touched our ears. Jesus strode by the sea, headed for his group of disciples. Another day of teaching and preaching appeared to be ahead.

Out of curiosity, I approached the group of familiar faces. They were a group of folks who were tanned and hardened by sun and wind, hands rough and calloused from the labors of a life of toil. The plain and simple folks I had grown up with, stood talking and laughing on the rocky shore.

"Peter, it would be a great day to cast a net," I greeted my old friend. He smiled and turned to Jesus who began to speak: "Today I am sending you out on a journey."

"But we have brought nothing with us for a journey," Judas protested.

"You will need nothing but the words I have given you."

As I watched, I saw a group of men who seemed most unprepared to go anywhere. Yet Jesus sent them out that day with the assignment to preach his words and he gave them the power to heal, to cast out demons, and to cure every affliction. I was astounded by what I heard.

"Go to the lost sheep of the house of Israel. And Proclaim as you go saying, 'The kingdom of heaven is at hand.' Heal the sick, raise the dead, cleanse lepers, cast out demons."

I saw the puzzled looks as the twelve whispered to each other with doubts and fears. I too, would have wondered, how could I carry out such a task. I looked at the group of plain-spoken men of the land and water, mostly Galileans, common folks like me, raised in these hills and on these shores. They were not clothed for a journey nor appareled to impress the people they met.

"What will we say?" Thomas asked.

Jesus told them not to worry, he would give them the words and the power. They were to go to the towns and villages and preach the words of Jesus. Jesus promised that they would know what to say. He promised they would be accommodated and housed by those they taught.

He had no promise that they would always be well-received, but if they were rejected they were to shake the dust from their sandals as a testament against such a town.

Peter stood up and told them that they could accomplish the task; that they had the word of eternal life and the power from God to peach and heal. Then I saw the flock of shore birds swirl around the ragged group and miraculously the men's faces lit up in smiles and laughter as they united in prayer and song.

As they departed, bound for various towns, I wondered how such zeal could fill these simple folks. They seemed to be possessed with some new authority. I thought I felt it, but then only fear and indecision crept into my thoughts.

Jesus walked towards me, with an intense smile that encompassed my fear, "Moshe, you will follow me. The power is yours too."

I could not respond and walked quickly and silently to my wood-working tools as the sun broke upon the smooth wooden side of the boat I was building.

Drawn close to sparkling Galilee,
Soothed and cradled by the suckling sea,
Building boats in the comfort of bustling Magdala,
Lulled to complacent quiet.
Healing Messiah, powerful,
Savior of the horribly possessed,
Followed by the hopeless, but now-forgiven, Blessed.

CHAPTER 21

By the Sea

Sometimes they left my beloved sea. My fisherman friends and Jesus would be gone for great lengths of time. Often, they ventured up to Jerusalem and the Judaean Lands. When my friends returned they told me of his preaching and his great works. He healed many and he preached in the temple at Jerusalem. He healed, even on the Sabbath and was criticized by the Pharisees.

John stopped by one day, "Jesus heals on the Sabbath. He says doing good on the Sabbath is perfectly in accordance with God's will."

"It seems to me that doing good is always in accordance with God's will," I reasoned out loud.

"The Pharisees are very upset with Jesus and say he breaks the law," John said.

"He brings a new interpretation and a new set of laws."

"He really upset the Pharisees when he chased the money-changers and sellers from the temple," John said with a worried look on his face.

"Moshe, when we enter the next Passover season you must accompany us to Jerusalem," John changed the subject for a moment.

"I will consider it," I said with little conviction.

"You must come with us, soon your boats will cover all of Galilee anyway."

"The sea is big enough for many more of my boats."

"You must see more of his great works and hear the words. Truly he is the Son of God, the Messiah promised to deliver us."

John went on with great seriousness, his eyes pleading for my full attention, "He refers to himself as 'the son of man,' just like us. We are sons of men. He takes his humanity seriously. How else could he be the Messiah except that he be one of us? He is sent from God to experience who we are."

"Yet his miracles and authority show him to be God," my mind was opened a bit wider as I began to see the connection of Jesus to God and men.

"Only a man could lead us and get our full attention."

"And only God could forgive and save us."

"I do believe this, but John, my boats...."

"No more important than my fish, Moshe."

As John turned to walk away, I realized how my little world by the Sea of Galilee had been changed. I still tried to focus on my boat-building, yet saw how my best friends had left what I thought was their only life and love, namely the fishing business. They had resolved to only follow the Teacher/God.

I had grown up with them just as I had grown up with so many friends by the sea. I remembered growing up with Mary from my home town of Magdala. Mary Magdalene, she was called in the circle of friends of Jesus.

Yes, I had grown up with Mary and had seen the horrors of her life, possessed by demons, her life was a shamble. She had been driven to many vices and a life of shame and ridicule. Every one had given her up as lost. As Jesus passed through Magdala one day, on his way back to Capernaum, He and his disciples saw her as she writhed in agony. Jesus had immediate compassion on her and cast the demons from her. He always seemed to be drawn to the most destitute of people and he always changed their lives to a life of forgiveness and compassion.

Mary and other women from the area had followed Jesus ever since, helping in his ministry and promoting his teaching. Mary's life had been changed, in fact life had been given back to her by Jesus' compassionate healing. Jesus' power over evil and his wonderful words of forgiveness had changed people and won their hearts and devotion.

Perhaps I too could be changed in such a way, but the sea and the boats still tugged hard at my heart.

Take us to the Mountain,
Jesus, change us, make us bright.
Take us to the Mountain, show us life and God's light.
Take us to the Mountain, preceding darker days,
Give us a glimpse of heaven
Before Jerusalem's haze.

CHAPTER 22

The Transfiguration

T here were days when I traveled with the group of Jesus' followers. I most remember a particular day and I wished for a long time that I had not been there. His words that day cut to my heart. I didn't want to believe what I heard.

Jesus stopped along the path toward Jerusalem, perhaps to emphasize to us the gravity of his words that day. The disciples sat around him to listen while I stood with others behind his chosen twelve. He spoke with with such fervor almost to the point of deep sorrow, "See, we are going up to Jerusalem, and the Son of Man will be delivered over to the chief priests and the scribes, and they will condemn him to death and deliver him over to the Gentiles. And they will mock him and spit on him, and flog him and kill him. And after three days he will rise."

I believed that the words and authority of Jesus must convince the church leaders, the scribes and Pharisees, and all the priests that he is truly the Messiah. I had seen the miraculous healing that Jesus accomplished. I heard and believed his words of repentance and his ministry of forgiveness. I knew him to be one of us. Jesus referred to himself as the 'Son of Man.' I knew him to be God by his mighty works, but I also knew him to be one of us, truly human, by his compassion and love for all of us. For me he held the special place of being a Galilean, a man who knew us, the fishermen, the farmers, and the craftsmen.

Then he broke my heart when he told us that he would be rejected by the church leaders and even arrested and killed because of his words. I had placed all my hopes in him and yet he said he could be put to death by the church leaders.

Peter my old friend went to Jesus and took him to task for even saying such a thing. Peter rebuked him, "Far be it from you, Lord! This shall never happen to you."

Jesus turned to Peter in anger, "Get behind me Satan, you are being a hindrance to me. You don't see God's plan, only what you want to see, only the plan of men."

Peter was crushed and I knew then that we did not see the whole plan. This was not about the worldly hopes of men for power and retribution of the Romans, but a plan that encompassed the whole world and all mankind.

Our hearts were broken, but how could we not follow him? He had taken us beyond anything we had ever hoped for, and now he told us we must take up his cross as we followed him to Jerusalem one more time. Indeed, we and many others would take up the cross.

My longtime-friend John told me of the days that followed. I had gone back to the sea; it was, as usual, my solace, my place to ponder, and perhaps my place to regroup my thoughts. John told me later of his trek with Jesus, James, and Peter, six days later, as they made their way west toward Mount Tabor. I wish I had known then what I now know, for this trek began to re-focus the leaders of Jesus' group. By their experience on the mount, they began to see more clearly the plans of God. The days were clear and bright as they passed vineyards and fields. Yet the specter of the mount grew as its green heights loomed in front of them.

I picture it in my mind just as John told it to me later. I see the four of them; Jesus and Peter, James, and John. The birds swirled higher and more abundantly than I had ever seen them. The four men walked with an excited gait. I heard them laugh and sing and share humor as they approached the mount. Their words and laughter uplifted my spirit after the sad predictions our Lord had shared with us.

John embraced my spirit with the strength of ten men, "Moshe, do not be afraid, do not be broken-spirited; Jesus is indeed our Messiah. We have heard and seen much these last days."

"I see that your spirits are high."

"Do not be dismayed, my friend, Moshe. All is well, rejoice with us." Nothing was said to me at that time of what they experienced on Mount Tabor, yet I felt an uplifting of my spirit.

Much later John shared with me the events on the mount. He told me how a cloud enveloped them. Jesus' face and clothes lit up like a thousand suns, so bright they could barely look at Jesus. Moses and Elijah appeared and conversed with Jesus. Then there was the voice. John spoke in reverent tones as he tried to describe the voice. He said, "Who can even begin to describe the voice of God? It touched our bodies and minds in a reassuring and peaceful way. Yet the power overshadowed everything." John said, we heard the words: "'This is my beloved Son, with whom I am well pleased; listen to him' and suddenly every word of Jesus spun through our minds and we knew him to be the one and only Savior of all."

Peter, of course felt the need to act immediately and volunteered to put up tents for Moses and Elijah and Jesus. Then Jesus touched them and they again felt normal as their friend and teacher spoke gently to them.

"We have listened more carefully than ever, since that experience on the mountain," John said, "and all that has happened has meaning beyond anything else in the world."

After the experience with Jesus on the mountain, John said that the focus of Jesus was fixed upon Jerusalem. His demeanor was set upon the upcoming days and events in Jerusalem.

Take us to Jerusalem, show us healing on the way,
Walk with Jesus and his friends,
In his enfolding love we'll stay.
We will follow his friends, his power we confess
Friends of Jesus and his followers will be eternally
blessed.

CHAPTER 23

Up to Jerusalem

The sea was again my comfort. The glistening waves soothed my soul to a certain extent. The familiar feel of my woodworking tools caressed my hands and put a sense of solidarity to my life; for a bit. I worked on a boat, even though I did not have an order for it. The shorebirds swirled in undulating patterns across the rocky shore and over the blue water of Galilee. I labored with my hands, yet my thoughts were with my friends and their teacher, Jesus. Truly the words played in my mind day and night and I longed to again hear them spoken by Jesus. Only his words could take my mind from the constant oppression of the Roman soldiers and their rigorous lock upon my beloved country.

I recalled how my friend John lately had actually referred to Jesus as The Word. Truly the lifeblood of his message was embodied in his words and those words touched us all to the depths of our spirit. And so, it was, that the hunger for those precious words called me back to that group of friends. It would soon be the Passover and I wanted to make the pilgrimage, I wanted to join Jesus and his followers as they found their way to Jerusalem.

I wasn't certain exactly where I would find Jesus and his disciples, but I decided to go to Bethany. I knew he had close friends there. Lazarus, Mary, and Martha lived there and they surely would be visited by Jesus as he made his way up to Jerusalem.

As I arrived in Bethany I soon learned that Jesus' friend Lazarus had just died. When I reached the home of Mary and Martha, there was great sadness and Mary and Martha had sent word to Jesus of their great grief. "If only Jesus had been here, Lazarus would still be alive," Mary wept as she spoke. It was a very sad day as we attended the funeral of Lazarus. With the mourners still gathered with the family, Jesus and his followers arrived.

The gathering was large. Many church leaders and other friends and relatives had come to attend the funeral of Lazarus.

"He will rise again," are the words I remember Jesus speaking to the sisters of Lazarus. We believed in the resurrection on the last day and believed the words of Jesus. Yet the teacher had other plans. As he neared the tomb, Jesus could be seen weeping with the other mourners. We knew him to be the Messiah, yet he wept with us at the tomb. Flesh and blood, he felt exactly what we felt. I realized again, at that point that he was one of us.

Jesus then did something that repulsed most of us. He had the tomb opened, even though Lazarus had been put into it four days ago. Some thought it a hideous request, yet perhaps Jesus wanted to see him one last time.

The voice scared me. I jumped in reaction to the loud command of Jesus, "Lazarus, come out!"

There before all of us, before the church leaders, before the friends and relatives of Lazarus, we saw a movement inside the dark tomb. We saw the burial clothes move and then appeared the form of a man. It was Lazarus, breathing and struggling to unwind himself from the clothes that covered his face and body.

Some cried in elation at the miracle. Others wept tears of repentance and joy. Yet I heard some murmurs in the crowd. Some had grim fears that this Jesus would topple their place in the

Roman bureaucracy. Many in the leadership of the church were protected and used for political advantage by the Romans.

Some of the disciples realized the danger Jesus was in, as he would be thought of as competition to the church leaders. Jesus' rise to fame could jeopardize the church leaders' position with the ruling Romans.

"We must leave and hide, lest they kill us all," Thomas the Twin rallied the disciples to flee the scene. My reunion with Jesus and my friends was hurried as we left for the rugged hill country of Ephraim.

Headed for the hills,
Respite from the crowd.
Friends, the greatest strength,
The people cheer out loud,
Palm leaves on the ground.
Upon a colt, Holy City bound
Messiah to the final bout.
Some shout, look to shields and swords,
But authority is in the words.
He sets his face toward the temple,
The holy ground, not for trading or profit-taking,
Here his authority shines, common sense,
Heavenly shaking,
Breaking earthly norms.
One of us,
He wields the power of life.

CHAPTER 24

The Fugitives

The word was out. I felt as if I were traveling with a band of fugitives. At times a silence fell over the group of Jesus' closest followers. The demeanor of Jesus had changed. The outreach and the healing were not his greatest focus. Now we climbed the rocky, barren outcrops of the hills. The dusty trails and rugged, thirsty plants clawed at our bodies and focused our spirits.

Jesus too, began to take on an attitude of rocky, craggy utility. His focus was now upon his core group of followers. His words were as hard and pointed as the country we traversed. He spoke of the temple in Jerusalem, "There will not be left here not one stone upon another that will not be thrown down."

He spoke of end times so troubling, "For in those days there will be such tribulation as has not been from the beginning of the creation that God created until now, and never will be." Times to come regarding those of us who believe his words, "Be on your guard. For they will deliver you over to councils, and you will be beaten in synagogues, and you will stand before governors and kings for my sake, to bear witness before them."

The most troubling were his words again, that were so hard to hear, as he spoke of his death, "For he will be delivered over to the Gentiles and will be mocked and shamefully treated and spit upon. And after flogging him, they will kill him, and on the third day he will rise."

These hard words were to prepare us for what was to come. Hard, rugged words, in the rugged hill country. Predictions that we all dreaded, yet the truth of his words would soon lead us to see the light of his life.

We now knew that the church leaders of the day were not the final answer. For us, his followers, his believers, the end game foretold was to be ours. For Jesus our Messiah will reign in eternity. We knew by the raising of Lazarus that we too had eternal life. After our rugged and most basic training in the hills of Ephraim, we headed back toward Bethany.

"We are in great danger to return to Bethany," one of our group said. Some followers left and returned to their towns. Yet some of us remained, determined to follow our Messiah where ever He would take us. His words had an authority that none of the church leaders could equal. Even as words of the high priest in Jerusalem, Caiaphas, spread through the country around us we followed Jesus. We knew there was a definite plot to capture Jesus. The leaders in Jerusalem feared the people as the following of the Messiah was growing.

Despite the growing danger, Jesus wanted to return to Bethany. He seemed determined to see Mary, Martha, and Lazarus again. There was an urgency and I got the impression that Jesus felt it would be the last visit to his close friends.

Martha as always, planned a fine dinner in Jesus' honor. Yet, the deepening lines on her face and the searching eyes, as she gazed upon her friend and Messiah betrayed her fears, as did her pre-occupation with food and planning. They were loyal friends and despite the growing danger from the religious leaders in Jerusalem they were intent upon honoring Jesus' presence. As we sat visiting with Jesus, always blessing us with his words of truth and life, Mary approached. She carried a flask of the finest imported aromatic oil. With the greatest humility she cleansed the feet of Jesus with the fine perfume.

Some of Jesus' closest disciples expressed disgust at the extravagance of treating his feet with such expensive oil. Of course, such oil could have been sold to benefit the poor. Yet Jesus expressed the greatest appreciation for the act, "She has done what she could; she has anointed my body beforehand for burial. For the poor you always have with you, but you do not always have me."

These were again, ominous words to my ears, for once again he spoke of his death. He seemed obsessed with the topic, and was much distressed at the implication.

Andrew expressed the same concerns that I felt, "There are those who would kill you and going to Jerusalem now is not wise." He spoke to Jesus. Yet Jesus was determined to go to Jerusalem for the Passover.

Despite the church leaders who threatened, there were great crowds of people who had heard the words of Jesus and saw his miracles. Now with the resurrection of Lazarus still fresh in their minds these followers prepared to give Jesus a very joyous welcome to Jerusalem. Many had heard the words of others who rebelled against the Romans, yet the words and actions of Jesus had won their hearts and minds. Some felt this might be the turning point when Jesus showed his great power and defeated the forces of bondage of our nation.

As I sat in the background, I listened as Peter, James, John, and Andrew discussed the next actions of Jesus and his followers. The plan was to travel to Jerusalem. Andrew stood to speak, "This is it, this is the time when Jesus will show his power to the church and to the Romans. We have seen his power, even over death, as he raised Lazarus, who can defeat him?"

"I would stand with him to the death," Peter stood and surveyed the others, "We need to hear his words. He spoke of the cross, so you say that he does not speak the truth when he speaks of the cross? You know what he is talking about, the Romans use their crosses to put down insurrections."

James urged them to hear John, "John speaks reason."

Now, as I tell this, I know what Peter, James, and John experienced on the mountain. They did not all see it in the same way.

"We must hear him, we must see how he will be the Messiah," John spoke quietly.

Andrew spoke loudly, "There are many who will support Jesus and will fight for him. He will enter Jerusalem as a king. No rebels have equaled him in power and authority."

"Now is the time," Peter stood by Andrew.

"Indeed, now is the time, as Jesus has indicated, but how it is to happen he will show us," James spoke in quiet testimony of Jesus' words. And so, with mixed feelings we followed although we were not yet sure of the path.

At that moment I thought back to a short time ago, when I stood on the shore of Galilee. I remembered how it had always been my custom to go to Jerusalem during the Passover. My family had always attended. The fishing stopped and we spent days in Jerusalem. John came by that afternoon, "Moshe, will you be going to Jerusalem?"

"I plan to attend the Passover, even though I need to get a boat completed."

"The Roman fish exporters become furious when we Jews stop fishing for Passover," John laughed, "but they depend upon us because no Roman would go on the water and catch slimy fish to export."

"It is possible to defy the Romans when money is involved; who else can they get to do the hard and dirty work?" I shook my head and laughed with John.

"We will travel with Jesus. Join us, Moshe."

At this point, my human instinct was to flee north to my beloved Galilee. I longed to sit on the rocks and hear the gentle waves, see the shimmering, dancing water, and smell the fish-scented shoreland. The words, the authority, the compassion, drew me to him. I followed, if only in the outskirts of his presence, never imagining any greater role than bringing up the rear.

Now as I rejoined the group of Jesus' followers, I remembered what a special journey it was to go up to the heights of the Holy City. Some of Jesus' disciples went ahead, for there were many in Jerusalem who had heard of The Teacher and wanted to hear more from him. Jesus spoke of his excitement to go before the church leaders and the people of Jerusalem.

"The people are clamoring to see him," Peter announced. "They want to hear him in the temple, feel his powerful authority, maybe experience his miracles."

"He must make a dynamic entrance to Jerusalem," Andrew followed his brother's lead. "Maybe a fine stallion and a sword; show them a leader and a king!"

"Lord, how will you enter the Holy City?" John asked calmly and in deepest thought.

"There is a colt waiting."

Some murmured in wonder and dismay, "Surely he could do better!"

On the first day of the new week, two of Jesus' followers returned from Bethphage leading a donkey and her colt. The colt followed its mother obediently.

"Place some coats upon the colt," James gathered the garments and gave them to the two disciples.

As the disciples raised Jesus up to ride upon the colt, it showed signs of nervousness, since no one had ever sat upon it before. As the colt stepped sideways and bucked in great terror the mother donkey came behind it and calmed the colt 's demeanor.

Now the Messiah reposed intently upon the colt. Someone remarked, "At least put him on the mother."

I remember Jesus' gaze upon the on-lookers, it was a gaze of total contentment and resignation as he surveyed the group. His eyes set upon Peter, James, and John, perhaps he trusted them in their knowledge of what was to come.

"We take the road past the Mount of Olives to the temple gate," Andrew spoke from the group.

Word had spread of Jesus' arrival in Jerusalem. Some had heard his words, seen his miracles, and believed his authority, and his Messianic legitimacy. I followed with some foreboding, knowing that those who sought to do harm to Jesus also were waiting in Jerusalem. Certainly, there were many people in Jerusalem who had come for Passover; folks from Galilee and the surrounding area. There were many friends and believers, but the sentiments of the religious leaders in Jerusalem were far different.

As I lagged behind our group of followers, I began to hear the crowds ahead. The sounds were those of people who were excited and joyous. The crowds lined the path to the city gate. The joy and singing pervaded the area as these believers welcomed their Messiah. My apprehension changed to wonder, as I realized the great support for Jesus. He was their Teacher, their Prophet, their miracle worker, and their God. The shouts of love and adoration filled the air and lifted my spirit.

Simon, the rebellious Zealot turned disciple, dropped back to walk with me, "See Moshe, this is what we have been waiting for. Look at the crowds, look at the support."

"Simon, you believe this is the beginning of a new kingdom, the fulfillment of all the prophesies?"

"I believe Jesus to be the Messiah as foretold."

"Such humility for one who is thought to be king," my questioning seemed to never stop, yet my spirits soared with the excitement of the day.

"He will go to the temple and his words will carry such authority that even the church leaders will listen and be convinced that Jesus is the Messiah. Of course, there is also his physical power. They must all be convinced and with their support the movement cannot fail." Simon grinned and lifted up his arms along with the crowd.

"I believe Jesus is the Messiah, I am not sure how it will all work out." I loved Simon's zeal but my own innate caution held me back.

For a moment, I rejoiced with the crowd, yet I saw the stern faces back from the road to Jerusalem. There were eyes that searched the reveling crowds, eyes that targeted the rebellious believers.

Jesus, protected and surrounded by his followers, entered Jerusalem and set his gaze upon the temple. Then I saw something that moved me to great wonder. Even in the midst of all the excitement and the rejoicing at Jesus' entry into Jerusalem, I saw the face of Jesus turn to a sadness I had only witnessed once before. I had seen his tears and grief at the tomb of Lazarus and now again I saw my Lord in a very distraught mood.

I wove my way between the excited and jubilant crowd, bumped into people, almost stepped on a child as he laid a palm branch on the road, and was finally able to approach Jesus. In the midst of all the rejoicing I saw tears in the eyes of Jesus. Even as he entered the city, he wept over it. His words sent trembling through my intellect as he spoke of the great Holy City being destroyed. In all its greatness, the core of the church rejected the words and miracles of the Messiah. He wept for them even in the middle of all the excitement by his followers from all over the countryside.

That day I saw Jesus experience the feelings of all people. From an outpouring of tears and heart-wrenching sadness over a people who rejected their loving teacher, to anger over misuse of the sacred temple by those only interested in financial gain. I gazed in awestruck wonder as my Messiah turned over the tables of those who cheated the people who had come to sacrifice. I knew that their exchange rates were greatly unfair and I knew first-hand how those who were given the right to charge money by the Romans made their exorbitant gains and paid off the Romans from their profits.

Jesus knew the temple to be a place for the words of truth; the reading of Holy Scripture and its explanation. Now Jesus' furrowed brow spoke of sadness and as he drove the commercial thieves from the holy temple, I saw not anger, but holy compassion for God's house and the people who truly sought God.

His words, "My house shall be a house of prayer, but you have made it a den of robbers," spoken to the sellers and traders as they left before his righteous wrath, required repentance.

I could see the wonder of some of those who looked on: 'What is he doing, those people are authorized by the government?'

Others murmured, 'But we know what dishonest criminals these people are.'

Simon Peter summed it up best, "Now he has everyone's attention, we will see who really supports him."

And so, I saw the crowds draw back, some in silence, others nodding. I knew that repentance and turning from sin would be his message as many gathered to hear his words. Jesus in the temple would solidify his following, prove his authority, or send some away in unbelief or believing they need not repent. And so, his time of teaching in the temple commenced.

I think that part of Jesus' appeal to many people was his gift for teaching from the everyday experiences of the common folks. His human plain-spoken stories kept our interest. Yet the message was the authority of God.

Jesus was not to be tripped-up in his own words; when one speaks, never wavering from ultimate truth, there can be no fault in his message. His words were from God, for he is God. On every point, as the church leaders tried to refute him, the truth of God always showed his authority. As he told the story of unlawful renters attempting to take ownership of property they were renting, he showed how he, God's son, was to be rejected and killed.

He pointed out a poor widow who gave her all to the church and elevated her above those who were wealthy church leaders.

I was spellbound as I heard his lessons, and I was terrified as he foretold the destruction of the amazing temple where he was teaching. His voice rang with authority as he told how not one stone would be left in place. We now know that he is the temple as are all believers and the physical building is not where we need to put our faith and trust.

Each evening, when he was done teaching, he retired, with many of his followers to camp and rest at the Mount of Olives, often going to Gethsemane in prayer. Again, as I had a few years earlier, I sat by a warming fire, speaking with Simon the Zealot.

"The authority and teachings of Jesus now dominate the discussions here on Olivet," Simon poked the fire and warmed his hands.

"There are those who believe he will lead a rebellion," I led into a touchy conversation.

"I once believed that Barabbas was the rebel who would lead us to freedom," Simon looked at me sincerely.

"Yes, but now as you know, he has been arrested and will probably be crucified by the Romans," I raised my eyes to meet those of Simon.

"I know now that the kingdom of our Messiah is not one of rebellion against the Romans; it is a kingdom of eternity. He has the power of Life eternal."

I came back with, "Jesus has said he will be lifted up. How can his kingdom endure his execution?"

"Do you remember our conversation some years ago at this very place? We spoke of the Prophet Isaiah and how he said the Messiah is to be like a lamb led to slaughter."

"Is this to be the end? Is he to be executed like all the other rebels?" I questioned softly.

"Look at the lesson of his friend Lazarus. Jesus has the power of life."

Simon was so changed by the words of Jesus. His skepticism of earlier days had become a faith that I still found difficult to totally comprehend. Some days I longed to return to Galilee, but I needed to hear and learn more.

Again, the next day I sat near Simon Peter and the words of the Lord terrified me. Never before had I so longed for the quiet shores of the Sea of Galilee. He spoke of the end times. I saw his gaze narrow upon Simon Peter next to me. His words of destruction fell upon our ears. Not only did he foretell the end times, but he painfully described how his followers would desert him. We had great tribulation to look forward to.

Again, that evening the fires on Olivet lit our night as many seekers of truth and possible relief from oppression spent the evening in quiet conversation. I looked through the early foliage and the smoky haze and saw the outline of an old acquaintance. I arose to greet him as he sat near the embers of a small cooking fire. I knew there was no mistaking him for his stature gave him away, "Simon of Cyrene, the Passover brings us together once again."

Rising to his full height, he looked down on me, "It is good to once again see a fine craftsman, Moshe. Sit by my fire and warm yourself."

We spoke of our common trade, the supply of fine building materials, and the newest techniques and fastening methods.

"So, Simon, have you been able to get near to Jesus of Nazareth as he teaches in the temple?"

"I have heard him from afar and plan to get closer. I have followed his ministry and learned of his notable authority. His teaching and miraculous works have brought me here."

"It will be a memorable Passover. Jesus has shaken the religious world of Jerusalem," I spoke to the Cyrene's questioning demeanor.

"You are from Galilee where he has taught so much and spends so much time. How has he moved the people?"

"His followers are many, but the Scribes and Pharisees here often openly challenge him."

"Yet, I heard he has met secretly with some church leaders who are open to his message, even open to the idea he is the Messiah."

"His message and authority go far beyond the people and the church leaders. His message is eternal."

"I don't understand what you mean by that."

I was surprised by my own words, "Listen to his words, believe his authority, don't be deceived by outward events. We must all be ready to endure great sacrifice in order to carry his message." I actually found myself pleading with Simon to keep an open mind.

Simon narrowed his eyes and stared into the fire, "We have all endured enough sacrifice with the Roman occupation of our lands. Where does it end?"

"Jesus says we, as followers, will have to take up a cross to follow him."

"I can't imagine carrying a cross to the place of crucifixion."

"You, Simon, know more about crosses than most."

"The Romans have caused us all to do strange and curious things to survive." At those words, I saw strain and distress in his firelight-reflected face.

"I have seen with my own eyes the power of his authority. It is authority of doctrine, authority of life, and yes, even authority over death. He is the resurrection and life itself. Simon, hear him, taste his authority and believe." I parted his fire and his presence, with solemnity as I too tried to grasp the true meaning of Jesus' words. My own words surprised me as I witnessed to Simon.

High feast, lamb and wine,
Prayer, Oh Father deliver me.
Words so intense.
Friends nod into the night,
Bellies full, drunken delight.
Prayer, Oh Father deliver me,
As torches flash friends wake,
Some flee.
A clash of steel, surrender.
Prayer, Oh Father deliver me.
Scattered friends in darkness,
Safe, not free.
A dark, mob-trial,
A night of horror.
Prayer, Oh Father deliver me.
People gather as they can see,
Morning light,
Mock-trial complete,
Barabbas will run free,
A cross awaits,
Prayer, Oh Father deliver me.

CHAPTER 25

Gethsemane

Jerusalem was abuzz. The Faithful had come from all parts of the known world to celebrate God's intervention into Jewish history. The Passover is a sacred celebration, the history of God's hand of deliverance for his people the Jews. I had learned the story from my youth and we have always made our way to Jerusalem to celebrate God's deliverance of His people.

The city and its residents enjoyed the busy time of Passover. Every possible place where people could gather to celebrate and remember God's grace was occupied, rented to those who came to visit. All the houses were filled with friends and relatives.

"Moshe, where will you celebrate the Passover?" Andrew asked as we left the garden the day before Passover.

"My relatives have a room where we will gather for the holy celebration."

"I am wondering where Jesus will gather the twelve of us who are close to him? We often wonder, yet Jesus always seems to have things planned."

"Peter and John said the Teacher had put them in charge of preparing for the feast; Jesus seemed to have preparations in place. He has kept the location quiet."

"We will be informed when the time is right. I understand the need for confidentiality, as there are many enemies who might want to disrupt our Passover."

So, I parted from Andrew and the twelve insiders who had now become Jesus' closest confidants and family. I looked forward to my own family and friends, promising to meet up with my Galilean disciples when they gathered after the feast.

Our family Passover meal was completed. We celebrated God's deliverance of our people from Egypt. As I thought of the history and the promises of the prophets, my mind wandered into the promise of a Messiah. Each Passover we are reminded of the promise and I wondered if this promise was indeed fulfilled by Jesus.

I had talked with other disciples about meeting later in the night after the meal and the remembrance. The feeling was that we'd meet at the Mount of Olives. Yet, I knew Jesus to be very fond of prayer at Gethsemane, so I went there first.

Seeing me in the dim light of a torch, Andrew ran up to me, "Moshe, come and join us, we have great concern."

"What is it, Andrew," I tried to put a consoling hand on his shoulder.

"Jesus has gone deeper into the garden to pray. He took Peter, James, and John with him and told us to wait here. "He seemed very troubled; I have never seen him so agitated."

"What do the others think?"

"Simon and a couple of the others are worried. Others have dozed off with heavy eyelids after the meal and the wine."

Simon the Zealot stood up and appeared very distressed. "Jesus spoke of betrayal and he seemed to implicate Judas Iscariot in a plot against him."

"Where is Judas now?"

"He left and seems to have gone ahead toward where Jesus is praying."

"As Jesus left for prayer, he looked physically drained, exhausted, and almost fevered," Andrew spoke with grave concern in his voice.

"Perhaps prayer is what he needs most right now." As I spoke, my attention was drawn to loud voices deep in the garden. The garden was usually a quiet place for meditation this late at night, yet the voices seemed excited and ominous.

Suddenly I felt the movement of feet on the rough ground and the smell of a lit torch as it flared when its holder swung around and faced the rising sounds. I was drawn along with the group of disciples as we moved rapidly toward the commotion. Even in the half-light of a torch I recognized Jesus, along with Peter, James, and John as a group of shadows moved toward them.

One of our group raced to the scene and excitedly embraced and greeted Jesus with a kiss. It was Judas Iscariot, who then backed away from our teacher as a group of men surrounded Jesus. There was the flash of steel and a scream of pain, then silence as we entered the circle of light. I saw Jesus calm the riot with his usual voice of quiet authority. "No more of this," as he then healed one of the high priest's servants who had been struck with a sword by Peter.

Then Jesus turned to the group of priests and officers of the temple who had come out against him, "Have you come out as against a robber, with swords and clubs? When I was with you day after day in the temple, you did not lay hands on me. But this is your hour, and the power of darkness."

One look at the ominous and well-armed group of elders and their servants caused us all to run. We disappeared and scattered in the darkness, yet Jesus remained with the captors.

I hid among the olive trees and watched as the flickering lights disappeared, headed toward Jerusalem. I felt helpless as my Messiah was led away, bound. I found my way to the Mount of Olives, checked the place where we met and found none of my Galilean friends. In terror and frustration, I headed toward the city.

Suddenly a hand touched my shoulder from behind and I whirled around to find John. "Moshe, I know where they have taken him. Peter has followed them. They have taken him to the high priest. He's being put on trial before the whole council. Peter is at the courtyard of the high priest now."

"So, we have all forsaken him."

"It seems true, yet Peter is following closely, perhaps the bravest of us all. He needs to be careful, for it was he who drew his sword against the high priest's servant. Even in the darkness they probably will remember him."

We carefully picked our way, rustling on the stones and cracked steps. As we approached the courtyard, I saw Peter talking to one of the servants. He seemed very agitated and suddenly left the courtyard, hurriedly without looking back.

We circled around in the darkness, trying to avoid being too conspicuous and found Peter weeping in the night. As we approached he turned to us and recognized us as friends, "They want to put Jesus to death! They have made false charges against him."

"Calm down, Peter. They will have to take him to Pilate, the governor, if they want to put him to death," John said in an effort to calm Peter.

Peter turned to me with a sadness in his voice I had never before sensed in him. "I betrayed my Lord just as he said I would."

"Peter, he will forgive."

"How, if he is put to death? We could have done more to save him."

Isaiah's words in Scripture played in my mind: "led as a sheep to slaughter, meek and mild, the lamb of God." The lamb of lambs, I thought. I had just eaten the Passover lamb and here was the complete sacrifice.

"He is the Messiah," I spoke to Peter with the greatest conviction I had ever felt, somehow gaining strength and a new feeling of resolution of my beliefs.

As we slinked near the courtyard, out of the reach of the firelight, we gasped at the horrible reality of what was taking place as our bruised and bloodied teacher was led out of the high priest's courtyard. Jesus' eyes met those of Peter as the early morning silence was broken by the sound of a rooster crowing.

"He saw me, he knows I haven't completely left the scene."

"They must be taking him to Pontus Pilate." John quickly evaluated what was happening.

"They intend to kill him," I reasoned.

"Let's follow, there may be something we can do." Peter quickly rose to his feet. We followed his lead, moving quickly and recklessly, fearless of discovery.

Just as suddenly we were stopped by something that we didn't understand immediately. We saw Judas Iscariot go into where the chief priests and elders had met.

"Why did Judas go into where the elders and priests have just met to condemn Jesus?" I stopped and shrugged at Peter and John.

"I suspect that the welcoming kiss of friendship that Judas gave our Lord was perhaps a sign to those who captured Jesus, to identify him in the darkness," John shook his head.

"Indeed, Jesus alluded to Judas being a betrayer," Peter spoke with contempt.

Shortly thereafter we saw Judas leave in a frenzy.

"The high priests certainly have not arrested Judas, who was known to them to be a close follower of Jesus," I reasoned. "and Judas seemed extremely distressed when he left. Things may not go well for one who has betrayed the Messiah."

From our distant view of the governor's palace we could see that Pilate was carrying on some sort of inquisition. Representatives and witnesses for the high priest seemed to have much to say. Jesus was mostly silent as charges were placed against him.

As the outdoor spectacle proceeded, a crowd began to gather, expecting a feast at the governor's courtyard.

"On this feast day the governor usually frees a prisoner to show good will to our people," John looked hopeful as the proceedings continued.

As the crowd grew we inched closer to the courtyard of Pilate. The governor seemed not convinced of Jesus being guilty of any wrong-doing, yet the priests accused him of blasphemy and also of being a revolutionary, one who would incite the people.

Pilate proposed that on this day of good will he would release Jesus. And then he gave the crowd a choice. He would release either Jesus or the revolutionary and known killer, Barabbas.

"Surely the crowd will not want Barabbas released," Peter excitedly pronounced.

"I have seen this revolutionary and experienced his incitement of murderous actions." I remembered the night at the Mount of Olives.

As the crowd went into frenzied discussion, the priests rallied for the release of Barabbas. Then I saw Simon the Zealot among the crowd, shouting to support the release of Jesus. Yet, the crowd had seemed to turn on Jesus. The tremendous support of the people as Jesus entered Jerusalem now seemed to turn against him. Some of the same faces that had shouted in triumphant support, now seemed to turn away. The bloodied and beaten Messiah seemed to no longer bring hope of a rally against the Romans.

Soon the loudest voices rose above the others and called for the release of Barabbas. I saw Simon the Zealot shake his head in opposition, even as he tried to convince many of his former associates and friends.

As Barabbas was released, much to his amazement, the temple leaders rallied for the death penalty for Jesus. The crowd turned ugly and chanted "crucify him."

Simon the Zealot saw us and rushed over, "Peter, Moshe, how can this be? How can this crowd support a murderous rebel and yell to crucify the one who had healed the sick and taught us the truth?"

"Peter and Simon, we must stay. Watch the entrance to see the verdict." I turned to watch.

Soon we saw Barabbas walk free, a man obviously guilty of crimes against the Roman Empire, was freed to walk away. A certain amount of incredulous shock seemed to emanate from him, yet he walked among the people, many of whom seemed to take comfort and even hope at his release.

"What of Jesus?" Peter looked to the Governor's palace.

"We must wait," Simon the Zealot staunchly looked to the entrance. "Can such an important decision be made so quickly?"

It was approaching mid-day when we saw Roman guards at the entrance. More soldiers exited and behind them followed the heart-breaking frame of our Messiah and teacher. Bloody, broken, each step seeming to be pure torture. Tied and led by a rope, or should I say pulled along, he stumbled and nearly lost his balance.

Thorns crowned his bleeding head, and purple bruises swelled on his arms. The words of the prophet: 'stricken, smitten, afflicted,' poured into my memory. Our prophet, our Messiah, was a suffering, broken, man.

Peter cried, "How can this be? We should have fought for him."

Then redemption came to me. "This is not a battle of this world. He has given himself to them. You know he could have escaped and defeated them, if he wanted to do it. He told us and we must watch and pray, and be prepared for him. He has the power over all evil, even death."

They led him to the street, the walk to the place of crosses and skulls.

Carrying it all, darkest day,
The world upon his shoulders lay,
Simon's cedar lifted.
Arms spread wide, nailed,
Some railed the King of the Jews.
Lifted up as women cried,
All sins defied,
A trembling world tried
To cover its shame.
The solace of a temporary tomb,
Escape the gloom
In the quiet of a peaceful garden.

CHAPTER 26

The Cross

I gasped as our Lord was pulled, bound, and stumbling to the street. "Like a lamb that is led to the slaughter," I recited the words of the prophet Isaiah. It all became clear to me now that this Jesus was the fulfilling Messiah spoken of by the prophets.

I winced at the long, bloody marks of the whip upon his shoulders and back, as Simon too recalled the prophetic words, "stricken, smitten by God, and afflicted...with his stripes we are healed."

In bitter tears Peter too recalled the prophetic words, "He was despised and we esteemed him not."

The words I had learned as a youth came to me in vivid recollection, "stricken for the transgressions of my people...he has done no violence and there was no deceit in his mouth."

We watched the horrifying spectacle of our Lord and Messiah. As the soldiers placed the heavy beam of the cross upon Jesus' back he was nearly crushed by the weight of the cross. It was then that I saw a familiar face, the face on a mountain of a man, yet a face downcast and saddened, for he had most intimate knowledge of the burden Jesus attempted to carry.

As soldiers prodded my acquaintance, Simon of Cyrene, the burly wood-worker lifted the cross with great familiarity and with anguish on his face hefted the cross onto his own shoulder.

Once again, he carried that wooden product of his own work-manship, followed by his Savior to the place of crucifixion.

We crept slowly behind the group of onlookers. Some came out of curiosity, perhaps to catch a glimpse of a miracle, or to see what all the commotion was about. Others went to Golgotha to view the hideous executions that were so common at the site. They didn't know the people being crucified and only attended as a diversion, an event to be viewed.

People came and went. Some, soon had their fill of the hor-rendous deaths being performed by listless, seemingly bored Roman soldiers. Others came because word had spread of Jesus of Nazareth being executed. These people had varied emotions. There were those who had hoped for a Messiah to deliver us from the Romans, and there were those who had been healed by Jesus or knew someone who had. Sadness, disgust, and tearful mourn-ing for a generous and loving teacher were expressed.

Our little group of Galileans huddled near the cross. We mostly all knew Jesus intimately. We had heard his teachings and tried, in our now-broken frame of mind to sort out the meaning of this day. We knew him to be a prophet, we knew him to have the power of life and death, yet we were confused about this day, which had descended upon us in such sudden and earth-shatter-ing fashion.

The day grew dark, not the dark of a storm that clouded the sun, but life-sucking dark that seemed to squeeze the light from the sun and darken us within and without. As three men strug-gled to keep the breath of life in their lungs, we spoke little and in muffled tones.

John, one of Jesus' closest friends, whispered, "I believe it is God's plan, but how could it be so terrible?"

I remembered that he told us 'the Son of Man must suffer many things and be rejected by the elders and chief priests and scribes, and be killed, and on the third day be raised.'

We could not comprehend these words, we were so convinced that he would prevail against the chief priests and scribes. Yet, he said he would rise from the dead. Peter and John just shook their heads in silence.

Then I saw him again. I moved to his side. His stature reduced to a stoop-shouldered man, head held low, tears in his eyes. Simon of Cyrene spoke in sobs, almost unintelligible, "I cannot go back to my business. I cannot do what I've been doing. The weight of the cross was so heavy, even I could barely carry it."

"It is not you who put him onto that cross."

"Moshe, it is all of us, we have deserted him, we have not repented, we have only carried on in the ways of this world."

"Simon, stay with us, there is hope and promise in his words."

Jesus, then, looked at John and asked him to care for his mother, Mary. The women huddled close to Mary and hugged her frail body. These women who had supported Jesus in his ministry, now were extremely shaken as they viewed his crucifixion. They were very distraught hoping for an immediate miracle and yet wondered how the body of Jesus could be cared for before the fast-approaching Sabbath.

Now, the very earth trembled and we knew the most important moments of our lives were upon us. We sat beneath the cross as the Roman soldiers did their appointed duty to ensure the captives were all dead. We knew that the Spirit of life had left Jesus' bloody, beaten body as he uttered 'It is finished.' The soldiers never broke the legs of Jesus as was often the custom. He was already dead. He had laid down his life and as a sacrificial lamb, no bones were broken.

"They seem to be done with their wicked work," John commented as the Roman soldiers left the crucifixion site.

"They would leave the bodies for the wild dogs," Peter lamented.

"What of our Lord's body? We are not prepared to care for it," I asked as I heard the wailing cries of the women.

"Who is that approaching?" John asked as he turned to the path up the hill.

"I have seen him often enough," Peter said as the man neared us. "He is on the Jewish Council."

"One of those who sent Jesus to the cross?" James quietly asked.

"I recognize him now. He is Joseph of Arimathea," John stepped toward the man.

"Have you come to see the work of your council?" Peter moved toward Joseph.

"I have come to take the body and prepare it for burial; I gave no consent for this deed of mis-justice. I, as you, looked to Jesus as our Savior. His words have touched my heart. I too look for the Messiah."

Upon hearing these words, Mary Magdalene came forward, "Where will we bury him?"

"I have a tomb in a garden that I have had prepared for my family. We can take him there," Joseph replied with a whisper.

Mary turned to the other tear-riddled women, "We must help to prepare the body for burial. The Sabbath is nearly upon us."

As Joseph took the body down, Mary Magdalene organized the other women to help. She worked with grim determination as one who had been saved, had her life changed by Jesus. She took charge, just as Jesus had taken charge of her life and saved it so miraculously.

Jesus' mother Mary looked to Mary Magdalene with tearful thanks, "Mary, you have become a true friend, and all your trials you have put behind you."

"Only my repentance and the forgiveness of my Lord could have made my life whole." The women followed Joseph and Mary Magdalene as they hurried to complete their tasks before the Sabbath began.

As Joseph and the women labored to prepare the body of Jesus for burial, I looked up at the two crucified criminals. Their lifeless bodies hung silent, as wild dogs growled with ravenous fangs gleaming in the waning day. Our little group of Galileans trudged in silence, not sure where we should go or how we should hide as the Sabbath crept upon Jerusalem. Even Peter walked with stooped shoulders in a silence I had never seen in him before.

No one seemed to know what to do next, as we found our way back to the city. Finally, John spoke to me, "Moshe, come and join us. We have a room where we can stay. We are prepared for the Sabbath."

"I have little thought for the Sabbath, right now, I have only a desire to rest by Galilee," I spoke as one dazed and utterly alone.

Jesus' closest followers were still, as a boat sailing on the Sea of Galilee that had lost all wind in a great calm, motionless and with no direction. We rested and prayed the prayer of the hopeless, yet his words still echoed in our minds. Even in the depths of our sorrow, his words sustained us. I remembered his voice: 'Truly, truly, I say to you, you will weep and lament, but the world will rejoice. You will be sorrowful, but your sorrow will turn into joy.'

I found comfort as I remembered he said: 'Behold, the hour is coming, indeed it has come, when you will be scattered, each to his own home, and will leave me alone. Yet I am not alone, for the Father is with me. I have said these things to you, that in me you may have peace. In the world you will have tribulation. But take heart; I have overcome the world.'

As we lay in hopeless exhaustion, his words had meaning that I now only began to comprehend. I had wondered at what he said: 'Nevertheless, I tell you the truth: it is to your advantage that I go away, for if I do not go away, the Helper will not come to you. But if I go, I will send him to you. And when he comes, he will convict the world concerning sin and righteousness and judgment.' His words and actions had never let me down before and now I believed his promises.

The Sabbath melted silently into the first day of the week. I remember the women's voices, loud but not wailing in sorrow.

They yelled excitedly and there was a joy that seemed almost surreal for me as the memories of the last two days still clouded my mind. Their words were unintelligible as I tried to bring my senses back to reality.

> The road goes back to Galilee,
> Charcoal on the beach.
> Repentance and forgiveness
> Beyond no sinner's reach.
> The road goes back to Galilee,
> The risen Lord appears,
> Brings life and his authority
> To everyone who hears.

CHAPTER 27

Galilee

On that first day of the week, I heard Mary Magdalene as she described seeing the risen Jesus. From the greatest depth of despair, I now heard joy. Her face glowed with excitement. Where tears had formed tracks down her face, I now saw an uplifted face, so clear and triumphantly excited. Peter too, spoke in new tones, not the grief of the day before.

The message that excited me was that Jesus would meet us in Galilee. "We must take the news of Jesus' resurrection home to our families," John looked to his fellow Galileans nearby.

Peter, looking ahead, "Some of us need to go to Galilee, it is our respite, but it is here in Jerusalem that we must continue the message of our teacher. He will tell us and lead us."

"He will meet us in Galilee," James referred to the message Jesus gave to those who saw him first.

The talk of beloved Galilee was all I needed to strike out immediately. I had always felt the love that Jesus had for our homeland on the shores of the great lake. A group of us headed out for home. I now traveled with hope. I knew I would see him there. His words had never failed to be proven correct. I began to see his plan more clearly. I had no idea what Jesus would say or do when I met him in Galilee but I happily set out for my beloved home.

Even if I moved quickly, it was a two-day journey. I usually made the trip a more leisurely trek, visiting with fellow travelers and stopping to rest my tired feet, maybe wash the dust from between my toes, and stop to eat lunch on the way. This time I kept a steady pace.

Some of my family traveled back, and yet instead of traveling with them, I found others who were in more of a hurry. Certainly, there was conversation as I traveled in various groups. The talk was often of the happenings in Jerusalem on Friday.

Some shook their heads and lamented the demise of a truly amazing prophet, "The church leaders conspired with the Romans to put him to death," one traveler spook with sadness in his voice.

"But I know people who saw him. He said he would be put to death and would rise again," I countered. Others had already heard news of Jesus' resurrection. Some scoffed and believed the reports that were circulating, about the body being stolen to make it look like Jesus had risen.

I believed what my closest friends had said and more over I believed Jesus' words. I knew he would be there in Galilee. So, I hurried my trip. As I stopped for water and to rest briefly, I once again encountered Simon of Cyrene.

"Moshe, we meet again," he greeted me.

"Simon, I am headed for Galilee. He has risen," I shared the message of my friends. "He said he would meet us in Galilee."

"I am traveling toward my home in Cyrene, I don't know what I will do."

"We must see him, we must follow him."

"For now, I will follow you Moshe, and see where I end up."

Often along the road I heard "Jesus" or another might utter "Messiah," while others shouted out against the Romans who had crucified Jesus. This news was stirring in the hearts of many who traveled back from the Passover. I could feel the emotion of the teacher's words and deeds spreading among the people. There was fire and great upheaval in the people. I wanted to pass on the words of Jesus and the growing assurance in my spirit that Jesus is truly the Messiah. I remembered he had promised the Spirit of Truth and help. I craved this and wanted the power of his Spirit to engulf me, lend power to my words.

Then it was before me, the blue waters of my homeland. I longed to reach my little abode by the sea and the solace it gave me.

Finally, I had returned. The time in Jerusalem seeming like an eternity. But now, I handled my tools, my wood-working implements. My hands caressed the smooth cedar planks, which I had readied for my next boat. The water kissed the rocky shore and I was, for a moment, moved to a peaceful reverie. I picked up a draw-knife and worked for a while, the grain of the wood seeping into my hands and caressing my spirit. I knew that this could no longer be enough. Yet, I longed for his voice of authority to once again fill me with a new zeal.

I slept by the sea that night, a sleep of deep rest. Peace had come upon me after the traumatic events in Jerusalem. I knew my friends had also returned to Galilee and I longed to connect with them once again, for they had seen my Lord. I knew that the fishermen brothers would all return to their familiar and their much-beloved waters of Galilee. Somehow, they would meet up with their risen Messiah.

As I awoke the sun was beginning to light the sparkling surface of Galilee. I could smell the scent of fish and water-plants. The shorebirds were beginning to feed upon the abundant life in the water. I wondered where I would meet the fisherman brothers. It took but a few moments to know how it would happen. I looked to the shallows along the shore and saw a boat so familiar to me, since I had crafted it. The occupants also were familiar; I could see the graceful cast of a net, spreading in a smooth circle as it hit the water. Only the skill of Simon Peter could initiate such a cast. Of course, the most normal thing for the fishermen brothers was to be on the water of Galilee in the first light of morning. They had put together a crew of seven of Jesus' closest disciples to go fishing. Even in the distance, as I watched, I could see the fishermen jerk the nets closed, yet bring them aboard empty.

As I sat by my shelter by the water, bare feet feeling the familiar stones of the shore, I caught a glimpse down the shoreline. It was a swirling white cloud, and I recognized a large flock of shorebirds reeling and soaring near the water. They continued to flash near the water, the clouds of white moving ever-closer to me.

Then I saw a form among the dipping and diving shore birds. The form seemed familiar as he chose his path carefully and stopped often to gaze upon the water. He paid particular attention to the fishermen in the boat. I watched as he gathered some wood and laid a fire on the shore. The basket he carried must have contained food for a breakfast by the water.

The fishermen slowly neared where the person tended his fire. I saw the flames flame high and then gradually calm down as coals formed for the cooking fire. As the boat neared him I saw what had to be the familiar, straight, and muscular form of Simon Peter, turn and release his throw-net upon the water. The circle of the cords glistened as the net arched into the now-rising sun. It was a lone cast, on the lakeside of the boat. I immediately saw the rope tighten and then others rushed to Peter's side to help pull the net. They seemed to strain as they retrieved the net.

I then saw a very strange thing happen as Peter turned toward the person on the shore, and then jumped out of the boat. Half swimming and then thrashing upright he headed toward the shore. For a moment I marveled, then I knew.

The person on the shore had seemed familiar and the shorebirds... Yes, it had to be Jesus. I then realized how he would meet up with his disciples.

Slipping into my sandals, I ran for the meeting, my heart longing to see my Messiah again. Breathlessly, I slowed and watched as they hauled fish to the shore and sorted them. The smell of fish cooking on the charcoals greeted my nostrils as I approached the fire. He turned and smiled to me and motioned for me to join them. As he motioned with his hands, I could see scars on both of his hands. They were the strong hands of a carpenter, and the wounds were ones that indicated piercing entirely through. They had been large, ugly wounds, now healed completely. I couldn't find words to speak as I stared at the hands, and then at the loving countenance of a teacher.

We broke bread and ate broiled fish with our Lord. It was a breakfast I barely noticed, hardly tasted as his words entranced me, the same words of authority that had led me to believe and now trust him with my life. He had words for each of us. He then spoke directly to Peter, who bowed his head in quiet contrition, not a typical action for him. Tears of remorse and repentance broke his composure and yet the words of Jesus were of forgiveness and compassion and his smile seemed to radiate and renew the great love and friendship between him and Peter.

Then he turned to me, "Moshe, this is a place you love and you always will, but now you will follow me, for you have the heart and the will of a builder, ready to tackle long and difficult tasks. I especially know the heart of a builder and you will now build my kingdom."

I then knew his words would carry me, and I longed for the Spirit he promised, to embolden my life for him.

www.ingramcontent.com/pod-product-compliance
Lightning Source LLC
Chambersburg PA
CBHW071222260626
47162CB00004B/1396